To
BOB & Kathy
Thanks for
support. May
continue to bless
Keep gou.
Sincerely -
Carl
12-9-17 .

MW01204720

LONG WAYS FROM *Home*

Ralph Carl Cannon

WESTBOW
PRESS
A DIVISION OF THOMAS NELSON

Copyright © 2009, 2012 Ralph Carl Cannon

All rights reserved. No part of this book may be used or reproduced by any means, graphic, electronic, or mechanical, including photocopying, recording, taping or by any information storage retrieval system without the written permission of the publisher except in the case of brief quotations embodied in critical articles and reviews.

WestBow Press books may be ordered through booksellers or by contacting:

WestBow Press
A Division of Thomas Nelson
1663 Liberty Drive
Bloomington, IN 47403
www.westbowpress.com
1-(866) 928-1240

Because of the dynamic nature of the Internet, any web addresses or links contained in this book may have changed since publication and may no longer be valid. The views expressed in this work are solely those of the author and do not necessarily reflect the views of the publisher, and the publisher hereby disclaims any responsibility for them.

Any people depicted in stock imagery provided by Thinkstock are models, and such images are being used for illustrative purposes only.

Certain stock imagery © Thinkstock.

ISBN: 978-1-4497-5622-2 (sc)
ISBN: 978-1-4497-5621-5 (hc)
ISBN: 978-1-4497-5623-9 (e)

Library of Congress Control Number: 2012910604

Printed in the United States of America

WestBow Press rev. date: 08/09/2012

To my mother Mary Alice Cannon, my wife Judith Marie, and to my granddaughter Natalie Rachelle.

And we rejoice in the hope of the glory of the Lord. Not only so, but we also rejoice in our sufferings, because we know that suffering produces perseverance, perseverance character, and character hope.

—Romans 5:3

CHAPTER I

In the land of Uz there lived a man named Job. This man was blameless and upright; he feared God and shunned evil

Job1:1

It was that time of day between late morning and early afternoon, and it had finally stopped raining. Not that it had rained so long—it had just rained so hard. It's like that in Mississippi. I was in Starkville, Misssissippi on the farm of Dr. David Lee Graves. Meharry Medical College was establishing a scholarship in his name and I was here to write a story on him and his family. I was met at the farm by a very friendly, little old man. I assumed that he worked for Dr. Graves. I explained to him why I was there, and he led me to a small cemetery near a pond on the corner of the property. I stood there in the private, little cemetery and watched the old man as he said a prayer and placed a bouquet of flowers on each of the three graves. When he finished, he looked at me. He seemed surprised that tears had formed in his eyes, and he wiped them away with the back of his hand.

"That's Doctor David's entire family," he said. "I kinda watch over things here. That there's his mother, Mary Alice; his father, Edward; and his brother, Douglas. They was real good people, but his mother, she was special. She was blessed with God's favor. When Mary Alice was a child, her mother use to tell her all the time how special she was. She told her she was blessed and had God's favor. She told her about me. How I would always be there to watch over her. She told her that if she were ever in need, if she ever lost her way and felt that life had gotten the best of her, she should call me. He momentarily closed his eyes and hesitated, then continued. "But when I was needed the most, all I could do was cry to the Lord like the others and pray.

"What happened to them?" I asked.

The old man wiped his eyes again, and then turned and walked away without answering. I leaned down and read each headstone, searching for an answer to my question. There was none. I turned and followed him to a little bench next to the pond. We both sat there silently; the old man as if waiting for me to repeat my question and me waiting for him to answer it. Finally he spoke:

"After her husband and child died, Mary Alice was never the same. She tried to let go of life, but God had other plans for her. God sent his angels, and through the angels he made a promise to her. She became a symbol of faith and an example of the power of prayer. Through her and her family, God showed that life is to be appreciated and lived to the fullest because of the suddenness with which it can be taken away. He showed the importance of real friends and that true love never dies. Most importantly, he showed that prayers are answered if you just believe.

"When God's promise to her was fulfilled, she came here one night to this little cemetery by the pond and simply let go of life. They found her the next morning, right here on this bench. Some say she grieved herself to death. Others say she was an angel and God took her home because her work here was finished. Either way, her life on earth ended right here on this bench. The doctor buried her here, next to her husband and her child."

A chill came over me and I could almost feel her grief. I could sense the agony of a wife suddenly losing her husband, of a mother losing her child, or the pain of anyone losing a friend or loved one and never fully recovering from the loss.

"What about her husband and her son? What happened to them?" I asked, repeating my earlier question.

The old man gazed up at the sun as if to get some idea of the time. He smiled and then looked at me as if time didn't really matter. "Would you like to hear a story?" he asked.

I turned on my recorder, opened my notebook, and nodded my head.

"It was during the time blacks were leaving Mississippi, the time of the Great Migration North. There were four of them: Mary Alice, Sophie, Lavern, and Minnie. They had been friends since childhood, and if you saw one, you saw the others. It was also about the time Johnnie B. arrived in Mississippi from Chicago."

"Johnnie B.?" I asked. I'd heard stories about him. "I thought he was just a part of Southern folklore."

"Nope," answered the old man. "He was as real as you and me, but I'll get to that later." He stared down at Mary Alice's grave and began his story.

It all started the day before Sophie and her husband, Johnathan, were to leave Mississippi for Ohio. Mary Alice, Lavern, and Minnie had come to say good-bye to their friend. Sophie stood in the doorway, staring out at her friends, thanking God for placing them in her life and for being so good to them all.

"Girl, you staring out of that door like you scared to come outside," said Mary Alice. "Come on out here and give me a hug. It's going to be a long time till we see you again."

Sophie smiled, opened the door, and stepped outside. The sun felt good. She reached up with both hands and stretched, enjoying the feel of the day. She slid a chair between Mary Alice and Lavern and sat down.

"We're going to miss you," said Mary Alice.

"Yes, we are," chimed Lavern and Minnie, in unison.

Sophie knew they were sincere. She understood because she was going to miss her friends too. She leaned forward, gave Mary Alice the hug she had asked for, and then hugged Lavern and Minnie.

"Now if you'll just take Mary Alice's little bad boys with you, we'll all be happy," said Lavern, and they all laughed.

The slamming of the screen door and the sound of children running interrupted their laughter.

"See what I mean?" said Lavern, and the laughter continued. Just as David ran by, Mary Alice jumped to her feet and grabbed him by his shirt. His brother, Douglas—or Doug as he was called—stopped as quickly as Mary Alice had stood.

"You kids know better than to be running through Sophie's house like that. What's the matter with you?" she asked. "Now run yourselves right to the road and straight home. Now get."

Doug darted for the road to avoid the swat on his behind that he knew was coming. Too late—she got him, anyway. David sulked away as if he had been the one swatted, so Mary Alice swatted him too, and he ran to catch up with his brother.

"Let me get them kids home," she said to her friends. She hugged each one, turned, and started down the steps. "I got to get them kids bathed, fed, and ready for church in the morning. Y'all going to church?" she asked Lavern and Minnie.

"No," replied Minnie. "I'm going to stay here and make sure Sophie's got everything packed and ready for when she leaves in the morning."

"Me neither, not this Sunday," answered Lavern. "I ain't got a thing to wear. Come on, let me give you and the kids a ride home."

"That's okay," answered Mary Alice. "Let them kids run some of that energy out, and Lord knows I need the exercise. This old girl can stand to lose a few pounds."

Lavern just laughed and shook her head. Mary Alice raised her hand, waved, and started after the kids. Lavern, Minnie, and Sophie sat there and watched their friend and her kids head for home. Tears started to build up in Sophie's eyes, but she was the oldest, the strong one. So she held back the tears—but not the emotion. They all watched Mary Alice as she and the kids disappeared from view. Their stares and the silence lingered.

It was Lavern who spoke first. "Lord, I'm sitting here like I ain't got a thing to do." Even though no explanation of what she had to do was necessary, she started anyway. She was like that. Sophie said it was because she was a hairdresser and always talking to customers about somebody's business. It wasn't criticism, just joking among friends.

"Jessie's about to close the barbershop, and I got to pick up the kids from Momma's," Lavern explained. "She's had them all day, and I know he's about tired. There just ain't enough time between work and sleep. I still need to do Julie's hair, unless Momma did it for me. If I can find something to wear, I'm going to church with Mary Alice." Satisfied with her unnecessary explanation, Lavern stood, turned to Sophie, and kissed her lightly on the cheek.

"You have a safe trip, make sure you write me, and send me a postcard. You know I like to get postcards from anywhere," she said. "Jessie and I will see you in Ohio in the spring."

She gave Minnie the same peck on the cheek, as if Minnie were going to Ohio with Sophie. Not wanting to leave but not having a choice, Lavern pulled her keys from her purse and headed slowly to her car. Once inside, she looked at herself in the mirror and wiped her eyes. She decided to pick up the kids first.

For some reason, she just wanted to see her kids, hug them, and tell them that she loved them.

Johnathan, Sophie's husband, was turning off the road as Lavern was entering it. Both cars stopped, and Lavern repeated the instructions she had given Sophie.

"Y'all have a safe trip; make sure Sophie writes and sends me a postcard."

Johnathan nodded. "You know she will. Tell Jessie I'll see him in the morning before we leave." They waved at each other as their cars headed in opposite directions.

Johnathan parked the car and tried to slow John, Jr.'s mad dash to his mother. Too late, John, Jr. stumbled, picked himself up, and ran to his mother. He pounced onto her lap and gave her one of those hugs so full of love that only a child can give.

"Say hi to Minnie," reprimanded Sophie.

John, Jr. climbed down, gave Minnie one of those same hugs, and said, "Hi."

Johnathan walked up to Sophie, kissed her on the forehead, and then turned and spoke to Minnie. "Minnie, how you doing? How's Sam? I ain't seen him in quite a while."

"We been fine," answered Minnie. "Sam's been working double shifts at the mill. I ain't seen much of him, either." She smiled. Sam was a hardworking man.

"The girls cooked us some food," said Sophie. "Seems like it's enough to last for a week."

Johnathan smiled and headed for the food. These women sure look out for each other, he thought. A good meal and some rest was just what Johnathan needed. He disappeared inside to get both. Ohio was a long ways from home and it would be a long drive. He would be ready, and so would Sophie and John, Jr.

Sophie and Minnie sat in silence watching the sun descend into the trees. It had changed from a brilliant red to a blazing orange. It was a beautiful ending to a wonderful day. The two of them talked through the evening and well into the night. They talked about the past in Mississippi and the future in Ohio. They talked about the reasons for leaving and the reasons for staying. They had all been born and raised in Mississippi and Mississippi was home. Minnie and Sam had decided to remain in Mississippi while Lavern and Jessie would be leaving for Ohio in the spring. As for Mary Alice, she and Edward were undecided. However, if it were up Mary Alice, she and Edward would probably be leaving in the morning with Sophie and Johnathan. They talked about their childhood friendship and how it had endured. They gave thanks because God had been good to them all and they knew it. Finally, they joined hands and said a prayer before Minnie bade farewell to her friend and headed home.

Early the next morning, after stopping at the mill to see Sam and saying his farewells to Edward and Jessie, Johnathan was ready to go. He had never been to Ohio, but the farm had been sold, and through an old army buddy from Ohio, there was a job waiting.

So, with his family and the acceptance of the unknown, Johnathan headed north.

CHAPTER II

Be still and know that I am God.

Psalm 46:10

*M*ary Alice fidgeted, trying to get as comfortable as possible on the hard church pew. *Lord, why don't they get some cushions for these benches?* she thought. Satisfied that she had achieved the best possible position, she closed her eyes, listened to the choir, and said a silent prayer for Sophie and her family. Just as she was about to continue her prayers and thank God for her blessings, a gentle tap on her shoulder interrupted her. She opened her eyes and turned towards the intruder.

"Wake up, girl" It was Lavern. Obviously, thought Mary Alice, she had found something to wear. "I just wanted to come say a prayer for Sophie and her family and hear what Reverend Johnson had to say to me today."

"How do I look?" she suddenly asked Mary Alice, as if expecting an honest answer.

"You look just fine," answered Mary Alice. She leaned over and gave Lavern a light hug.

Satisfied that it was an honest answer, Lavern fidgeted on the hard bench just as Mary Alice had. Finally, she crossed her legs, leaned back, and decided to do her best to endure. The hard bench and the mid-morning heat would surely test her endurance.

The church was unusually crowded, and Mary Alice wondered if all these people were here to pray or to be prayed for. She glanced at her husband Edward sitting next to her and at Lavern's husband Jessie. They were in the group to be prayed for, she decided. She chuckled at the thought. As if sensing both the glance and the thought, Edward turned to Mary Alice and smiled. He was a good man, a hardworking man, and they loved each other dearly. She returned the smile, softly squeezed his hand, and said a prayer of thanks to God for bringing them together .

Edward and God both seemed unusually attentive today, so she continued her prayers of thanks. She said a prayer of thanks for bringing Edward safely home from the war. She said a prayer of thanks for her children, Doug and David, whom she called her "little bright spots." She said a prayer of thanks for her friends and their friendship. She said a prayer of thanks because God had been good to her and she knew it.

A loud "Amen!" brought Mary Alice's attention back to the singing. The choir was finishing its song, and Lavern was obviously ready to hear what God had to tell her. So was Mary Alice, but right now she was more interested in God helping her get Edward to move to Ohio.

"Good morning," said Reverend Johnson in that deep, rich voice that sounded as if it came from two people. He stood there, opening his Bible and waiting for a reply.

"Good morning," echoed the congregation in unison. Mary Alice fidgeted again. She reached out and pulled one of the little cardboard, wooden-handled, hand-held fans from the slot in the pew in front of her. She hoped that it would at least make the heat a little more tolerable, but she knew better.

"It's so good to see so many people here on this first Sunday of the month," continued Reverend Johnson.

No wonder there were so many people here, thought Mary Alice. It's the first Sunday. She had been so preoccupied with Sophie leaving and with Edward's indecision, she had totally forgotten that it was the first Sunday of the month.

Mary Alice and the rest of the congregation finally stopped fidgeting. The whispering stopped and it grew quiet. Reverend Johnson bowed his head, closed his eyes, and silently asked God to bless and protect his congregation. He always asked for God's blessing and protection before each sermon, and today was no exception. God always seemed to oblige him.

"Amen," said Reverend Johnson, as though he had prayed out loud.

"Amen," repeated the congregation, as though they had heard him pray.

Reverend Johnson looked up, closed his Bible, and took off his glasses. Today what he had to say was not only in the Bible, but in his heart. He was seventy-two years old. Life had taught him a lot, and he wanted to tell the congregation some of what he had learned. He knew that many of them would be leaving Mississippi, and for some of them, leaving had been a tough decision. Still others could not or would not decide. Could he make them understand that there would be tough decisions in life and sometimes, regardless of the choice they made, there would be consequences? He knew that a great change was spreading across America, and his congregation could be part of that change or be swept up in it.

Change is never easy, but change they must. The one thing he knew for sure was that they could not be afraid of this change. There was no place for fear. Faith was required, a fearless faith. Whatever they did or wherever they went, they should not make decisions or live their lives based on fear, but on faith. They should not be afraid of the consequences because God was in charge.

He looked around the crowded church, at the faces filled with anticipation. Could he make them understand, he thought, almost out loud. Could he make them understand that it is possible to live a life free from fear, free from anxiety, free from confusion, free from indecision, a life loving God? Could he make them understand that through faith all of this was possible? Would they? Could they understand? "Surely someone would," he whispered.

"Fearless faith!" he almost shouted. He waited for a few long moments and then, in that same reverberating voice, he continued.

Tough decisions!" Again he paused, this time as if waiting for some sign to continue. A soft "Amen" from somewhere deep in the congregation seemed to be what he was waiting for. In a voice that was a little softer, drawing the words out a little longer, he simply said, "Knowing God is in charge."

Mary Alice sat listening intently, thinking maybe God was trying to tell her something. Edward sat with that same expectant expression as Mary Alice and Lavern. Maybe God was trying to tell Edward something too, she thought.

In a voice that now sounded like a prelude to some good singing, Reverend Johnson continued. "A great change is spreading across this country, and we can be a part of this change, or we can be caught up in it. Decisions have to be made, tough decisions, decisions that will have consequences. Some of those consequences will be basic and simple. Some will seem harsh. Others will seem almost unbearable, but that's the price that life and change sometimes demand."

A soft, almost inaudible "Amen" escaped from Edward's lips. Mary Alice heard it and repeated it, followed by a small chorus of amens from the congregation. Lavern was silent. Everyone seemed to sense the sincerity and urgency in Reverend Johnson's voice.

He continued, "But we cannot live in fear of change or in fear of the consequences of our decisions. We must live in faith—a strong faith, a fearless faith, a faith strong enough to override the fear of losing everything. We should not, we cannot, and we must not live in fear. We must realize that God is in charge and be not afraid."

There was a louder chorus of amens from the congregation. Reverend Johnson paused to let the words sink in. The chorus of amens continued.

"We must be thankful for our blessings, not fearful that they will be taken away," he said. Scattered applause joined the chorus of amens.

Mary Alice fanned herself a little faster with the almost useless cardboard fan. She thought back to her earlier prayers of thanks. Yes, she was thankful for her blessings, but she knew that she was fearful of losing those blessings. Wasn't that a natural feeling, or was that an indication of a lack of faith? Mary Alice sat there wondering, listening and momentarily confused.

Reverend Johnson continued, "Thankful not fearful, faithful not doubtful. Faith in God, faith in ourselves... faith in our spouse... faith in our children... faith in our people... faith in our decisions... faith in our families... faith in our future... Faith! A fearless faith. A faith that will be tested, of that you can be sure, but God has promised us that no more shall be put upon us than we can bear." The amens and the applause continued. A few people stood.

Mary Alice closed her eyes, searching for an answer to the dilemma Reverend Johnson had presented. If tested, would her faith fail her, or would she fail it? Was such faith possible when it came to losing everything?

"Speak Lord, speak to me," Mary Alice whispered. She momentarily turned to Edward as if expecting an answer. What was God telling him, she wondered.

Her gaze returned to Reverend Johnson, and he continued his message on faith, of living by faith. He told them of Enoch, who by faith was taken from this life and did not experience death. He told of Noah, who by faith built an ark to save his family when warned of things not yet seen. By faith Moses' parents put him in a basket, knowing God had a plan. By faith the walls of Jericho fell after the people had marched around them for seven days. By faith the people passed through the Red Sea as if on dry land. He told them of the prostitute Rahab and her faith. Because she welcomed the spies, she was not killed with those who were disobedient. He spoke of Gideon, Barak, Samson, Jephthah, David, and Samuel. He told of the prophets, who through faith conquered kingdoms and gained what was promised.

The longer he spoke, the more Mary Alice began to realize the truth in his words of faith. Finally she understood. She understood decisions would have consequences, but God was in charge, and through faith all things were possible. She understood that there would always be some fear of losing those things that she cherished the most. Regardless, her faith would be stronger than her fear. She would make her decisions and live her life based on faith, not fear. She would trust in God, because God had been good to her and she knew it.

The heat and humidity were starting to take a toll on Reverend Johnson. After almost two hours, he was emotionally and physically spent. He wiped his brow, put on his glasses, and reached for his Bible.

"Fearless faith," he said. Opening his Bible to the book of Job, he started reading at chapter 1 verse 19.

"Then Job arose, and rent his mantle, and shaved his head, and fell upon the ground and worshipped and said, 'Naked came I out of my mother's womb, and naked shall I return thither; the Lord hath gave and the Lord hath taken away; Blessed be the name of the Lord.' In all this Job sinned not, nor charged God foolishly'. Fearless faith," said Reverend Johnson as he closed his Bible. "Fearless faith. May God add a blessing to the reading of his Word."

Having given all that he could give, Reverend Johnson turned and walked to a large cushioned chair reserved especially for him. As one of God's angels, he had been instructed to deliver a word directly to a chosen few. He looked out at Mary Alice, so highly favored by the Lord. She was one of those chosen few to whom he spoke. He quietly said a prayer for her and her family. He knew that, like Job, her faith would soon be tested. She would lose so much, but God through his grace and his mercy always gives more than he takes. She would eventually be blessed far more than she ever dreamed and become an example of the awesome power of prayer.

"Amen," whispered Reverend Johnson.

"Thank you, Jesus!" a voice shouted from the back of the church.

"Yes Lord!" shouted another.

Gradually the praises subsided and calm settled over the congregation. The choir's final selection signaled the ending of the services. Mary Alice and Lavern clapped their hands in appreciation of the message delivered by Reverend Johnson. Edward was silent. Finally the benediction was given and the services concluded.

"Girl, Reverend Johnson sure can make you feel good about yourself," said Lavern, trying to stand as gracefully as possible after sitting for so long.

So that's what Reverend Johnson had to tell her, thought Mary Alice. Everyone seemed to have received what they needed from the sermon. For some it was simply some quiet time away from the daily confusion in their lives. For others, the issues were more complex.

"Come on, let's get the kids," said Mary Alice. She pulled Lavern along and pushed Edward.

"Y'all go ahead. I'll meet you outside," said Edward. "I just want to speak to Reverend Johnson."

"Wait," said Jessie. "I'll go with you."

Mary Alice watched Edward and Jessie walk away, wondering what God had told them. Maybe Ohio was in her plans after all. Regardless, Edward was her husband, and if it was God's will, she would remain with Edward in Mississippi. Even so, her heart was set on Ohio.

Just as Mary Alice and Lavern turned down the aisles toward the children's classroom, the children appeared, trying their best not to run. Mary Alice put her arms around Doug and David and asked them what they had learned in Sunday school. Lavern did the same to her children, Julie and Alfred. All four children tried to answer at once.

"They must have really enjoyed class today," Mary Alice and Lavern said to each other, before laughing at their sudden, similar thought. As they left the church, the children's urge to run returned. Mary Alice and Lavern decided to let them. The sun and the temperature had both reached their peaks. The heat, coupled with the humidity, would not allow them to run long. A few people lingered outside, mostly discussing who was leaving Mississippi going where. Mary Alice avoided those conversations but was her usual polite self.

"Edward and Jessie sure got a lot to say to Reverend Johnson," said Lavern. She and Mary Alice walked over and sat down on a little bench under the nearest shade tree. A soft breeze made their little shady spot almost comfortable.

"You know how they get. It's like they're brothers talking to their father when they talk to Reverend Johnson," said Mary Alice.

"Ooops, looks like we talked right up on them," said Lavern. They both laughed as Jessie and Edward invaded their little shady spot. Edward seemed somewhat nervous, occasionally wiping his forehead.

"We been trying to talk Edward into going to Ohio," said Jessie to no one in particular but looking directly at Mary Alice.

"Come on man, not now. We'll talk about it later," said Edward, also looking at Mary Alice. "Doug and David, let's go!" He shouted, as much to change the subject as to call the kids. Jessie understood and issued the same order to his kids.

"Ed, I'll see you later this week," he added.

The heat and humidity had tired the kids enough that they were waiting at the cars. Mary Alice gave a departing wave, telling Lavern she would see her Thursday or Friday to get her hair done.

"We need to talk," she said as they drove off.

CHAPTER III

In his heart a man plans his course, but the lord determines his steps.

Proverbs 16:9

The kids had finally gone to sleep, and Mary Alice stood in the hallway trying to decide whether or not to do the same.

"Hey you," whispered Edward as he walked up behind Mary Alice and gave her one of those little hugs that she liked so much.

"Hey you," she replied. She knew that was his way of saying that he was in the mood for some affection or some conversation. Either one was fine with her, but right now she hoped it was some conversation about leaving Mississippi.

"Let's go out on the porch. I want to talk to you," he explained.

I just bet you do she thought. "Go ahead, I'll be right there. Just let me check on the kids," she said as she tried not to hurry. "Go ahead."

Mary Alice watched Edward for a few moments as he headed for the kitchen, then she turned and walked across the hallway to the kids' bedroom. The door was partially open as always. She walked in, closed the door, and waited for her eyes to adjust to the darkness. After her little visual adjustment, she glanced at the kids then looked around the room, inspecting it for anything out of the ordinary. Satisfied that all was as it should be, she walked over to the bed and sat down next to her tired, sleeping children. She reached down and pulled the covers over them, more out of habit than to keep them warm. She kissed each one of them on the forehead and said a prayer for being so blessed. It was something she did every night. This was her quiet time with her children, that time that solidifies the bond that can only exist between a mother and her children.

Mary Alice sat silently in her quiet world, wondering what the future held for her children. If the family moved to Ohio, how would the change affect them? If they stayed in Mississippi, how could she possibly prepare them for the future that was so rapidly approaching? She thought back to her own childhood that had come and gone so quickly. Like her children's, it had been filled with love, hope, family, and friends. It had been filled with the things, places, and people that would mold and shape her and become an integral part of her life forever. *May God bless those people.*

Then the war came and went, as did those people. At seventeen, her childhood had all but ended. The war was over, Edward had returned home safely, and they were married. A year later, her oldest son Doug was born. Two years later, after the birth of their younger child David, it became apparent to her that the family's future was not in Mississippi. She told Edward that the future was dependent on the children, and she did not want to raise her boys in Mississippi. The lack of educational opportunities and the danger alone was enough for her to decide that Mississippi was not the place to be.

It was just in the last few years that she had decided on Ohio. Sophie and Johnathan had gone there for the jobs. Lavern and Jessie had originally decided on Chicago, but then decided that a smaller town in Ohio would be a better place to raise their children. Also, the fact that it would be cheaper to open their business up north was enough to convince them that Ohio was the place to go. All of this appealed to Mary Alice and she wanted desperately to follow her friends north.

The movement of the curtains from the breeze blowing in the window caught Mary Alice's attention and brought her thoughts back to the children. She walked over and pulled the shade down but left the window open. *Lord, I don't want the sun waking them kids up with the chickens,* she thought. She walked back over to the bed but sat down next to it. By now her eyes had completely adjusted to the darkness and she could clearly see the children.

"Eight years old and you looking more and more like your daddy every day," she said, gazing down at Doug. "And you looking more and more like your brother," she said as she looked over at David.

She sat there, again wondering about their future. They were good kids and Mary Alice, like all mothers, hoped that they would one day grow up to be good men with children of their own. Then, as a grandmother she could start the whole wonderful process over again. Standing and almost laughing out loud at the thought of being a grandmother, she decided she was getting way ahead of herself. First things first, she would go see what Edward had to say.

Edward had grabbed two of the kitchen chairs and taken them out on the porch with him. He sat down, stretched out his legs, leaned back, and stared up at the night sky. It was a clear, beautiful night sky. It seemed like all the stars were shinning right over Mississippi. He sat there, alone with his thoughts, listening to the sounds of the silence of a Mississippi night. It had been an emotional day for him, and the peace and quiet of the moment was just what he needed. He glanced back at the door, hoping

Mary Alice would provide him with a few more minutes to enjoy this solitude.

Reverend Johnson had been right, he thought. A change was spreading across America, but wasn't Mississippi part of America? Wasn't change needed in Mississippi? Wasn't a change in the way black children were educated in Mississippi needed? Wasn't a change in the living conditions of black people in Mississippi needed? Wasn't a change in the way black people were treated in Mississippi needed? Wasn't Mississippi a part of America, or was change avoiding Mississippi altogether?

With all the changes needed in Mississippi, leaving and going to Ohio had been a tough decision for Edward, but one that had to be made. He wanted to remain in Mississippi and help make some of those changes. He knew that change could not avoid Mississippi forever. He also knew that if he stayed or if he left, there would be consequences. He didn't consider the consequences of his actions as Reverend Johnson had said, rather the opportunities provided by them. It was time. It was time for a better education and a brighter future for his children. It was time to realize their dreams and take part in this great change that was spreading across America. It was time to leave Mississippi.

"Hey you," whispered Mary Alice. Edward was almost startled. *It's a good thing she didn't shout,* he thought. *She would have scared me half to death.* He almost laughed out loud but only smiled. How long had she been standing there and how long had he been sitting here, he wondered. This time he did laugh, only softly.

"Hey you," he replied as expected. "Come here."

Mary Alice stepped outside and sat down next to him. She slid her chair as close to his as possible, then leaned over and kissed him softly on the lips. Stretching out just as Edward had, she leaned her head back and stared up at the star-filled sky.

They sat there, holding hands like school kids, enjoying the warm night, the gentle breeze, and each other's company. Mary Alice started to speak but decided against it. After all, she reasoned, he was the one who wanted to talk. She would remain silent and wait. The seconds turned into long minutes and still they sat, each thinking of the other. As Mary Alice had hoped, Edward spoke first.

"I've been thinking about what Reverend Johnson said today," he said. Just as Mary Alice was about to respond, Edward continued, "For a while there in church, I felt like I had you in one ear and Reverend Johnson in the other, and both of y'all telling me to leave Mississippi."

"So," interrupted Mary Alice. "What's wrong with that? You going to listen to me and Reverend Johnson, or you going to be your usual stubborn, hard-headed self?" She had to laugh at the accuracy of her description. Edward laughed too because he knew that he could be stubborn.

"What I'm going to do is listen and then do what makes you happy," he said with a smile.

That is so sweet, thought Mary Alice. She could actually feel herself blushing.

"You were right when you said our future wasn't in Mississippi," he said. "The future is the children and children's future is education. Unless there is a change in Mississippi, they won't be able to get the education and learn what they need to know if they stay here. They need to learn what white kids learn. They need to learn that all white folks ain't bad. They need to learn what they are instead of what they ain't. They need to learn that they can grow to be strong, educated, confident black men in charge of their own destiny and not ruled by small groups of racist white folks. I don't think they can learn those things in Mississippi. Maybe in Ohio, but not in Mississippi."

"Thank you, Jesus," said Mary Alice. "He finally understands that this is not the place to raise our children." Mississippi could be a very harsh and dangerous place for young blacks trying to become men. Even after black boys reached manhood the dangers remained. For outspoken black men like Edward, the dangers were ever-present. His father, like her parents, had been a victim of the hatred and the fires that burn late at night in the small towns of Mississippi.

"Reverend Johnson was right," said Edward. He stood, walked the few steps to the edge of the porch, and once again stared up at the star-filled sky. He turned to Mary Alice and continued, "This change ain't going to happen overnight. It's going to take a long time, two, maybe three generations. See, we don't need to change the way white people act, we need to change the way they think. If we can change the way they think, then maybe they'll act like they got some sense. It might be their kids or their grandkids, but somewhere along the line they have to understand that we can all live together, that we're all Americans. Maybe it will happen in Ohio, but not in Mississippi. So, you're right; it's time we leave Mississippi."

"Tonight?" joked Mary Alice.

"No, not tonight," laughed Edward as he sat back down.

"I know," said Mary Alice, a little less lighthearted and a little more serious. "It's just that it's so good to know that we're finally going to leave Mississippi."

"I know," said Edward. "I know."

Again they sat there in silence. Suddenly Edward stood up, took Mary Alice by the hand, and pulled her to her feet.

"Come on," he said.

"Where are we going? To Ohio?" she asked.

She laughed as she followed Edward down the steps and out into the yard. They walked across the yard towards the gate that led to the barn and the pasture. Even with the light from the moon and all the stars, it was still quite dark. *Where in the world are we going*, wondered Mary Alice. Just as they crossed the path and reached the gate, Edward stopped. He stood there with one foot on the gate, looking out over the field. Mary Alice stood there waiting for answers to the questions she wanted to ask.

"Well?" she finally asked.

"That," said Edward pointing out over the field. "That's almost two hundred acres of prime land. Most of it's been in the family for a long time."

Mary Alice turned and interrupted him before he could continue. "Don't tell me you're going to sell the land?" she asked with more authority in her voice than she intended.

Edward noticed and quickly explained. "Not all of it," he said. It was more to reassure her than to answer her question. "We'll rent the house out, and I'm going to sell Sam a hundred acres down by those woods near his place. He'll look after the rest for us. Sam knows why we're selling it, so he gave us a good price and said we could buy it back any time we want. We got to keep the land because that's the one thing white folks can't make more of. One day in America they're going to run out of room. He'll send us some money once a month until it's paid for. That and the rent will give us a regular income until we can get a restaurant started in Ohio. He was hoping we would stay, but he understands."

"What about the restaurant here?" asked Mary Alice.

As if anticipating the question Edward answered almost immediately. "I'm going to sell the restaurant. Reverend Johnson said there's a couple from Greenwood who want to buy it. We'll sell it next spring before we leave."

Well, thought Mary Alice, that answered her next question too. She had hoped they would leave sooner but she knew he was right. She would be patient and wait. Whether they left tomorrow or next year, she now knew they were leaving and that's all that mattered. She always had faith in him to do what was best for the family. Now, God willing, life in Ohio would provide for them what life in Mississippi would not or could not provide.

Mary Alice walked over and leaned against the fence next to Edward. She put her arm around him and laid her head against his shoulder as if to assure him that he had made the right decision. She wanted to let him know that all was right in their world. Edward turned and hugged her to him to let her know that he understood. They were like that. It's late," she whispered.

Edward held her in his arms a moment longer. He looked into her eyes as if he had more to say, but simply smiled. He took her hand and they started back across the path towards the house. A small group of clouds had gathered and were spread thinly across the sky, not enough to cover the stars but enough to make them twinkle. The breeze was blowing a little harder but it was still a very pleasant evening.

"Looks like it might rain," said Edward, mostly to himself.

Mary Alice didn't respond and Edward barely noticed. They continued on in silence. Just as they reached the house, Edward stopped, turned to Mary Alice, and asked, "We happy?"

Again she felt herself blushing and she answered, "We very happy."

CHAPTER IV

Sing to the Lord a new song
For he has done marvelous things.

Psalms 47: 7

hree months had passed since Edward's decision to leave
Mississippi. Not much had changed, with the exception of
Mary Alice's enthusiasm for leaving, which had grown daily. The
children had reacted to the news of moving as expected, with
curiosity and questions. Any excitement was merely Mary Alice's
perception caused by her own feelings.

Edward, the ever-dutiful husband and father, simply worked
longer and harder to best prepare his family for the move.
Mary Alice, the enthusiastic wife, did all she could to help. Her
weekdays were divided between the children and helping Edward
at the restaurant. Her Saturdays were spent doing everything else.
Sundays there was church and, if possible, some rest. The coming
months would require more and more of their time and energy.
Regardless, they knew that when all was said and done, it would
be worth the effort.

Edward had gone from indecision to total commitment. Not
that he wasn't always totally committed to bettering their future,
but now he had a new direction. He viewed this as a new chapter
in their lives and he anxiously looked forward to it. He joked with

Mary Alice that he didn't know who to thank, her or Reverend Johnson.

"Just thank God," she would reply. "Just thank God."

Today was Saturday, David's birthday, and Mary Alice had decided to be still and get some much-needed rest. She tried unsuccessfully to get Edward to do the same, but as usual he insisted on working.

"Don't work too late," she said as she followed him to the door.

"I won't," he promised. "I saddled the mare for the kids and I'll bring a cake home for David."

They stood in the doorway, Mary Alice toying with the top button of Edward's shirt, again pleading her case for him to stay home. Realizing the futility of her efforts, she gave him a quick kiss and as she had done so many times before, watched him walk out into the early-morning darkness to the car.

"I'm going to have to do something real special for that man one day," she said.

She walked to the kitchen to get a cup of coffee. She loved coffee in the morning. She told Edward it was what kept her looking good for him. With her deep, dark, rich color so like her coffee, and a lock of curly hair constantly hanging down over her light brown eyes, she really was quite an attractive woman.

The children and the sun both seemed to have awakened at the same time, so Mary Alice decided to go out on the porch and watch one and listen for the other. Coffee in hand, she walked onto the porch, enjoying the feel of the cool, crisp morning air. She sat down on the porch with her legs and feet dangling over the edge.

The heat of summer had finally succumbed to the fall, and the mornings were cooler but more enjoyable than ever. She pulled the sweater tight around her shoulders, as if to contain the warmth provided by the coffee and the rising sun.

I sure wish my man was here with me, she thought as she watched the sun rising above the treetops. The early morning darkness had given way to the to the dawn, and the sudden brightness with its vivid colors surprised her. Today, the usual yellow of the sun was splashed with orange and streaked with red, making her momentarily doubt what she was seeing. Any doubt quickly turned to appreciation as she stared, captivated by the colorful spectacle in the sky. It was as if the sun had malfunctioned and the brightness and all the colors were unintended.

"What a beautiful start to a new day," she said. She bowed her head and thanked God for providing it. "Good morning, Mr. Sunshine" she whispered. She glanced upward one last time and started toward the door.

"Good morning, kids!" she shouted as she walked back inside. The kids, like the sun, were now fully awake. "Good morning!" repeated Mary Alice after getting no response from her initial greeting.

"Good morning!" shouted Doug as he stepped aside to let David run to his mother.

It's my birthday! It's my birthday!" he shouted, his personal declaration of a new day. It was as if the world had started on the day he was born and everyone needed to be reminded that today was a celebration of that glorious event. Jumping into his mother's arms, he gave her a big hug and a kiss, then hugged her again.

"What was that for?" asked Mary Alice.

"Because it's my birthday," answered David.

"Yes, it is," said Mary Alice. She returned the hug, put David down, and held out her arms for Doug. He had waited patiently, knowing that his hug and his birthday were both coming.

"Hi, Momma," said Doug as he wrapped himself in his mother's outstretched arms.

"Hi, baby. How you doing this morning?" she asked as she gave Doug a little extra squeeze.

"I'm fine," answered Doug.

"Good, now y'all go get washed up and come get some breakfast," she said as she started for the kitchen. "We're going with Lavern to see Minnie, and I don't want you getting there and telling me how hungry you are. Doug, go look on the porch and get my coffee, please."

"Yes ma'am," answered Doug.

"And make sure your brother washes good," she added.

"Yes ma'am," came Doug's automatic reply.

With the exception of David's birthday, breakfast proved mostly uneventful until David got started. He was as talkative and happy as any just-turned six-year-old could be while his brother was unusually quiet.

"Did you see the sun this morning?" David suddenly asked. He obviously was as surprised by the beauty of the sunrise as Mary Alice was by the question.

"Yes I did, honey. It was beautiful," she answered, unable to contain the smile his question had so innocently caused.

Doug remained silent. *What is on that child's mind,* wondered Mary Alice. She watched him staring down at his plate, toying with his food. Unlike David who was a constant bubbly bundle of joy, Doug was more reflective and more serious.

"What's wrong, Doug?" she finally asked.

"Nuthin'," he replied.

"Are you sure?" she asked.

"He don't want to leave Mississippi," volunteered David.

"You don't know nuthin'," said Doug, raising his head and his voice.

28

"That's enough," cautioned Mary Alice as the boys glared at each other. *When did all this start,* she wondered. She thought they were excited about leaving. "What's this about you not wanting to leave Mississippi?" she asked, returning her attention to Doug.

"David said that, I didn't, and I do want to go to Ohio, it's just that…" his voice faded to a whisper, then silence.

Mary Alice waited then asked, "Just what?"

Looking at David then back at his mother, he asked, "Are we ever going to come back to Mississippi?"

So that's it, thought Mary Alice as she leaned back in her chair. She wasn't surprised by the question because she had asked herself the same thing more times than she cared to count. Unable to answer it to herself, how could she possibly answer it to an eight-year-old and a just-turned six-year-old who had so inadvertently started this whole discussion? She wanted to tell him that this was not the place to be, but she knew that was not what he wanted to hear. He didn't need her to tell him again about more opportunities and better education in Ohio. What he needed to hear was the answer to his question. She didn't know the answer so she decided to tell him the truth.

"I don't know, honey. I just don't know," she said. There was silence.

"You're gonna miss Mississippi, ain't you?" she asked. She stood, walked behind Doug, and placed her hands on his shoulders.

"Kinda," answered Doug.

"You want to know something?" she asked as she ran her fingers through his short curly hair.

"What?" asked Doug. He looked up at his mother and wondered if she understood how he felt.

"We're all going to miss Mississippi," she replied. She understood. With the exception of a few trips with Edward to buy horses, Mary Alice and the kids had spent their entire lives right there in Oktibbeha County, Mississippi. The Southern way of life and open spaces had become a part of them. Leaving Mississippi would not be as easy as she thought, but this was the journey the family had decided to take.

"I'm gonna miss the dirt roads and the sound of gravel on the car," she said as she walked back to her chair and sat down. "I'm gonna miss the pond down by the woods and my little table and bench."

"I'm gonna miss fishing in the pond," said Doug. He felt better knowing that maybe they understood.

"I'm gonna miss the horses," said David, simply glad that everyone was once again happy.

"I'm gonna miss the horses too," added Doug. "Mamma, can we ride Old Cliff over to Miss Minnie's?"

"No, no, nooo. Y'all leave that crazy horse alone. Your daddy saddled Lady for you before he left this morning, and that's gonna have to do," she answered.

That's fine, thought Doug. With David riding with him, it was best that they rode the mare. Doug was a little uneasy trying to ride Old Cliff but he was always willing to try.

The mere mention of horses had the kids ready to go.

"May we be excused?" asked Doug, standing as he spoke.

"Not till you finish your breakfast," answered Mary Alice.

Minutes later, they were again standing and asking the same question.

"Go on. Get out of here," said Mary Alice after inspecting the empty plates. "Y'all be careful and stay on the path," she shouted to the kids as they ran from the kitchen and out the door towards the barn.

Once outside, they slowed to a walk and stopped at the gate. They stood there, staring at the horse tied near the barn as if they were two Goliaths looking at David instead of two small children about to take control of a thousand-pound horse.

"There she is, David, all bridled and saddled and ready to go. Go break me a switch and I'll get the box," said Doug as he headed for the barn. Even with the saddle it was difficult for them to mount a full-grown horse. To make it easier, Edward had made a box for Doug to stand on. It allowed him to reach the stirrup, mount the horse, and pull his brother up behind him.

Mary Alice decided the dishes could wait and went outside to check on the kids. She walked over to the gate and sat on the top rail of the fence. She braced herself and watched the kids go through their practiced routine.

"One day I won't need this box," said Doug. He placed the box on the ground, untied Lady, then led her into position. Edward had taught them from the beginning that the left side of the horse belongs to them and the right side belongs to the horse. It was a valuable lesson and one that Doug and David both remembered well.

"Here, hold these," he said to David and he handed him the reins. Stepping up on the box, he grabbed a handful of Lady's mane with one hand and the saddle horn with the other. He placed his foot in the stirrup, pulled, and he was on. Once he was seated firmly in the saddle, David handed him the reins and the switch then stepped on the box. He grabbed his brother's outstretched arm with one hand, the back of the saddle with the other, and pulled. It was a quite a struggle as always, but finally he was on. Reaching back, Doug pulled his brother a little closer to him. He nudged Lady in the side, tapped her hindquarter with the switch, and they were on their way.

Mary Alice sat there watching them as they followed the path away from the barn and out towards the pasture. "Y'all be careful and go straight to Minnie's," she shouted as David looked back and waved. She returned the wave and repeated her instructions.

Doug tapped Lady again with the switch and she tossed her head and picked up speed. David wrapped both arms around his brother's waist and held on tightly. Now, fully in control, Doug rode along the edge of the pasture, following the path that led to the woods. From there it was a short ride to Minnie's house. All thoughts of Ohio and leaving Mississippi were now completely forgotten. Today they were in Mississippi, happy and doing what they loved and did so well.

The sound of Doug and David's laughter hung in the air as Mary Alice watched them disappear into the woods. Could they possibly be this happy somewhere else doing something different, she wondered. She knew that once they left Mississippi life was going to be different. Living on the farm had enable her to shelter the kids from most of the harsh realities of the world. With hundreds of acres of land to roam and horses on which to do it, they lived in their own little world. Their world was structured and full of love and they were happy. Now, she wondered, was it right to sacrifice this for what she hoped was a better future in Ohio that was not guaranteed?

She understood that life required sacrifice, but was she sacrificing too much? At what point does a mother give up her children's happiness for the chance of a better future for the family, she thought. If they aren't happy as children, can they ever truly be happy as adults? She sat there somewhat confused. For the first time she had thoughts of trying to change things in Mississippi and finding happiness at home. Was that possible? She did know that the real world extended far beyond the boundaries of the farm. She knew that eventually her children would have to leave the farm for the real world. Was now the time? Should she disrupt their life here for an uncertain life such a long ways from home? Had she really considered the children's happiness, or was she merely caught up in the changes sweeping across the country, the migration North, and the pursuit of some unfulfillable dream?

She shook her head as if trying to shake some sense back into it. Yes, it was possible, she decided. It was time for change. The decision had been made. Regardless of the consequences, deep down inside she knew it was time to leave Mississippi.

"Get it together, girl. You can't sit here all day," she said. She laughed at herself. She looked up at the sun to get some idea of the time. Lavern was going to be there soon, and she hadn't done a thing but sit there on that fence. Even so, it really was a good day for just sitting. Sitting there on that fence uselessly trying to predict the future, she had barely noticed the beauty that surrounded her: the lush greens, the deep blue sky, and the bright golden sun.

Suddenly she could feel it and it felt good. She stretched, leaned back, and enjoyed the sun as it warmed her body and deepened her deep, dark, rich color. Swaying back and forth, she softly hummed the tune of her favorite song. The sun disappeared then reappeared from behind one of the few clouds in the sky and her humming continued. Finally, climbing down from the fence and walking back to the house, the humming of the tune became the words to the song, softly at first, then increasingly louder. Walking a little faster, she raised her hands to the sky and began to sing.

> *He touches me in the morning and blesses me with a new day.*
> *He puts peace in my mind and joy in my heart and washes all my troubles away.*
> *I'm grateful for all he's given me and I'll do all I can to show it.*
> *I'll lift my voice and sing his praise, because God's been good to me*

And I know it.

Yes, God's been good to me and I know it.

CHAPTER V

A man of many companions may come to ruin
But there is a friend who sticks closer than a brother.
Proverbs 18:24

Mary Alice had finished the dishes and her second cup of coffee when Lavern arrived. *Late as usual*, thought Mary Alice as she walked outside to greet her friend. Sophie and Minnie jokingly called her "Late Freight" because she always seemed to be late. It wasn't as though she had been blessed with the gift of procrastination; it was just that she always seemed to be late. Something always happened or something always came up. Even Lavern had to laugh at the name, and there were times when it seemed she wore it with pride.

"I know. I know. I'm late," she said. She took one last look in the mirror at her hair, smoothed her blouse down, and stepped from the car. Mary Alice sat on the porch with her feet once again dangling over the edge. She waited and prepared herself for Lavern's long explanation as to why she was late.

"The kids decided they were going to spend the weekend with Momma," she started. "Ain't that something, they decided. And Momma don't make it no better. She should just keep their decision-making behinds twenty-four seven."

Lavern walked up on the porch, pulled a chair next to her friend, sat, and continued her explanation.

"I told them today was David's birthday, and they acted like they didn't hear a word I said, so I took them straight to Momma's. Then Momma wanted to sit and talk. I told her I should have been here an hour ago. Ain't that something, they decided? So where's your kids?" she asked, satisfied that her lateness had been sufficiently explained. "I thought David would be running out here to remind me that it was his birthday."

"Oh, he'll remind you," said Mary Alice. "Edward saddled one of the horses for them and they rode over to Minnie's. They just like their daddy when it comes to horses. I don't know what they gonna do when we leave Mississippi. We can't take horses to Ohio with us." Mary Alice stared down at the ground, then looked at Lavern as if she wanted to say more, but she remained silent.

Lavern waited, then finally asked "You all right?"

Mary Alice stared back down at the ground then asked, "'Vern, are you ever coming back to Mississippi?"

Lavern laughed. "Girl, I ain't never coming back here. That's why I'm leaving, 'cause I don't want to be here." She expected Mary Alice to join her in a moment of lightheartedness.

But Mary Alice didn't laugh. Instead she repeated her question. "Are you ever coming back to Mississippi?"

"What's wrong?" asked Lavern. She realized something was troubling her friend.

"This morning at breakfast, Doug asked me if we were ever coming back to Mississippi and I didn't know what to tell him," she answered.

"So what did you tell him?" asked Lavern.

"I told him the truth. I told him I didn't know, and I still don't know," she said. In all her childlike innocence, the simplest things seemed to perplex her the most. Lavern understood that about her young friend.

"Look, let me tell you something" said Lavern. She leaned forward and placed her hand on Mary Alice's shoulder. "It's simple. Yes, I'm going to come back to Mississippi because Jessie's coming back, if only for a little while. You're going to come back because Edward's going to come back. This is where they're from. They were born here and they'll probably be buried here. Mississippi is a part of them just like it's a part of us. It's in our blood and you can't change that. That's why Jessie and Edward keeping all that land. 'Course, Jessie sold some to get us started in Ohio, but he got enough to come back to. When he comes back I'll come back, and you'll do the same with Edward. We all need to remember where we're from. If you don't remember where you're from, you'll never know where you're going in life. So girl, get that old sad look off your face and tell Doug that he'll come back to Mississippi."

Lavern started to continue but decided to wait for some reaction or response from Mary Alice. Mary Alice shook her head, smiled, and pushed herself from the edge of the porch to the ground. "You always know what to say," she said. She grabbed a handful of rocks and started tossing them one at a time towards the road.

Although she was only two years older than Mary Alice, Lavern was more worldly and had a certain wisdom that Mary Alice lacked and so often benefited from. They were true friends and they understood each other.

"Come on, let's go," said Mary Alice as she tossed the last rock. "I need to make sure the kids made it to Minnie's in one piece." She felt better and Lavern could see it. She felt better because she finally knew the answer to Doug's question. Little did she know it was a question that he would never ask again.

"Yup, that's right. We'll be back," she said. She opened the door and climbed into the car with Lavern. Leaving would be easier now that she knew she would be back. As for the kids, they would be all right, she thought.

"You want to try driving today?" asked Lavern as she turned the car from the drive onto the road.

"Nope, not today," answered Mary Alice. She rolled the window down and leaned her head back to enjoy the wind blowing through her hair.

"Girl, when you going to learn to drive? asked Lavern. "You need to learn to drive before you leave Mississippi."

Mary Alice didn't respond. She simply turned her head to the side and let the wind blow the curls across her face. "Don't worry," she finally answered. "I'll learn to drive once I get to Ohio. You sound just like Edward."

"You plan on doing a lot in Ohio," said Lavern. She tried her best to sound irritated but was unable to do so.

"Yes, I do," said Mary Alice. "Yes I do." She hesitated for a moment, then continued. "I want to go back to school." She looked at Lavern as if seeking her approval. "Remember when we were little and the Klan burned the school down?"

"I remember," answered Lavern. "We were all there. You, me, Minnie, and Sophie. After the fire we had to go to school in the church. Then we was scared they was going to burn the church down with us in it. It was real bad times," she said as she reflected back on the sadness of it all.

"I never owned another book since then except the Bible," said Mary Alice. "I remember we stood there and watched the school and all our books burn and wondered why. I thought they were just mean people." She paused, remembering the fire, the smell of smoke, and the charred remains of what was once the start of their educational future. "I should have never stopped going to school," she said. She turned her head and gazed out of the window at the passing countryside and at the spot where the school once stood. Lavern could only agree, partly because what Mary Alice said was true and partly because she didn't want to dampen her young friend's dreams.

They spent the remainder of the ride laughing and joking about the future in Ohio. They laughed about the cold weather and building a snowman. Just the idea of a snowman amused Mary Alice more than anything else. She was still laughing when they turned from the road and stopped in front of Minnie's house.

"Do they build snow women," joked Mary Alice. She shook her head and ran her fingers through her hair to make herself at least presentable.

"No, girl. You got to do better than that," said Lavern. She reached into her purse to get Mary Alice a comb. "You need to come by and let me do something with that hair. Why don't you let me cut it down some?"

"Edward would have a fit," answered Mary Alice. She pulled her hair back into a ponytail and secured it with a rubber band. "A snowman," she said, almost in disbelief. She laughed as she climbed from the car to go find her children.

"Hello," shouted Minnie. "Come on out here in the back." With the dirt roads and gravel, it was hard to arrive unannounced in Misssissippi.

"I'm serious," said Lavern. You need to let me do something with that hair."

"Whatever," said Mary Alice, refusing to comment or carry on any futher conversation concerning her hair.

They followed the sound of Minnie's voice to the rear of the house where Mary Alice hoped to find her kids. Instead she found Minnie seated at a table snapping beans. Mary Alice sat down and grabbed a handful of beans, more to have something to do than to give any help. Lavern sat down, leaned back, and watched.

"The kids are out by the barn with Sam," said Minnie, anticipating Mary Alice's question.

"I hope they ain't been no trouble," said Mary Alice almost apologetically.

"Girl, those kids ain't never any trouble. They're always welcome here. Sam stayed home from work today and the kids coming over was the best thing that could have happened to him." Just the thought of it all brought a smile to Minnie's face. In one of life's cruel ironies, Sam and Minnie, who loved children so much, could have no children of their own.

"I tried to get Edward to stay home too, but he didn't want to hear it. It's like he can't do anything but work since we decided to go to Ohio," said Mary Alice as she pushed a handful of beans toward Lavern.

"Here, make yourself useful."

Lavern frowned and reluctantly grabbed the beans. "Jessie's the same way," she added. "He's been working like that every since he came home from the army. All three of them just working and buying land. Always talkin' about one day white folks in America gonna run out of room. They got such big plans," she said, a bit of sarcasm in her voice.

"Oh, you don't have plans?" Minnie quickly asked. "If you don't, you should. We all should. If we don't, things ain't never gonna change. Ain't that why you going to Ohio, 'cause you got plans?"

"Well, I got plans," said Mary Alice emphatically.

"I hope you plan on learning to drive," joked Minnie. They all laughed. Mary Alice was almost as well-known for not being able to drive as Lavern was for being late, though the distinction had yet to earn her a nickname.

"I'll be driving before you know it," answered Mary Alice. "I told 'Vern that this morning. Then I'm going to go back to school, get a job, and buy me a car." She leaned back in her chair and folded her arms across her chest to emphasize her point. Minnie and Lavern laughed as though Mary Alice had just spoke of doing the impossible.

Minnie just shook her head, marveling at her young friend's enthusiasm. She had seen the same enthusiasm in Sophie when she decided to leave Mississippi. Though Sophie's plans were more thought-out and more detailed, the enthusiasm was the same.

"And what about you, Miss Lavern?" asked Minnie. "What do you plan on doing in Ohio?"

Lavern looked at Minnie as though she were insulted by the question. "Ain't no secret," she said. "Everybody knows what my plans are. Me and Jessie going to have a beauty shop and barbershop on every side of town. You know how people up North like to dress up and look good. Come to think about it, we might even have us a cleaners or two." She tried her best to sound modest, but she meant every word she said.

"What about you, Minnie? Don't you want to leave?" asked Mary Alice. Before Minnie could answer, Mary Alice continued, "What about Sam, can't you get him to leave?"

"Girl, Sam ain't going nowhere," answered Minnie.

"Then what about you?" repeated Mary Alice. "Don't you want to leave?"

Minnie looked at Mary Alice not quite knowing how to answer. She thought for a moment, then tried to explain. "None of us want to stay in Mississippi, except Sam," she said as she tried to force a smile. "You know how bad it is here; that's why you leaving. But some of us can't leave."

"Or won't leave," said Lavern. She suddenly wished she hadn't spoken.

Minnie continued as if Lavern's wish had been granted. "I want to leave, but go where and do what? Me and Sam, we're farmers. Sam ain't going North to work in some factory. He just can't do it. He can't. Neither can I. Sure, Sam works in the mill, but to him that's a part of farming. They pay him a fair price for the timber on our land, and he gets paid for working at the mill doing what he likes to do. Me, I'm just Sam's wife and I gotta stay with my man."

"Don't you see?" she asked. She leaned back in her chair, not really expecting an answer. "I can't leave. My life is here. Some of us do what we have to do instead of what we want to do. Maybe if I had kids things would be different," she said wistfully.

Minnie has always been that way, thought Lavern. Even when they were kids and the school burned down, her attitude was one of acceptance. She felt that the burnings and the killings were an inevitable part of life for black people, just as she now seemed resigned to her place in life in Mississippi.

"You know," Lavern stated reluctantly. "One day they going to close the mill. They been talking about it for years. Then what?"

"Well," sighed Minnie, as if the closing of the mill was one more acceptable hardship of life in Mississippi. "Me and Sam talked about that. Sam has always been careful with a dollar. With the milk cows and the land, we'll get by."

"Get by?!" asked Lavern a little louder than she intended. *Get out*, she thought. Lavern wanted to scream the words. *How can she sit her, shoulder the burdens, suffer through the humiliation and tolerate all the abuse,* she thought. *What about life—her life?* "Get by" meant just to survive. It was a saying Lavern had always heard from Minnie and she hated it. She wanted to tell her that there was no life here. She wanted to tell her that life was not meant to be lived under these conditions in this horrible place. But as much as she wanted to, she knew it was not her place to tell her friend how or where to live her life. She suddenly felt embarrassed by the implication and only hoped her friend would forgive her for her intrusive behavior.

Minnie sensed Lavern's embarrassment and smiled a forgiving smile before leaning forward in her chair. "Besides," she continued in a low whisper, as if she were about to reveal some deep, dark secret. "By the time the mill closes, America will have run out of room and all that land will be worth a fortune. Then Sam can buy the mill."

She said it clearly and calmly, as if it were some well-thought-out plan. Then, looking directly at her friends, she raised her hands, leaned back, and laughed out loud, as if it was the most outrageous idea ever dreamed up. They all laughed until their eyes watered. They laughed partly because it was the most outrageous idea ever dreamed up, and partly because in the back of their minds, they all thought it was quite possible.

"You silly," said Mary Alice as she stood and looked toward the barn for her children. "Let me get those kids. I know they're out there getting on Sam's nerves."

"Girl, sit back down," said Minnie. "Them kids ain't going nowhere. Besides, we don't see a lot of each other since Sophie left. Don't rush off; y'all gonna be leaving Mississippi soon enough."

"Yeah, but we'll be back," she said as she sat back down and slapped hands with Lavern.

So they sat there in the early afternoon warmth of Mississippi, laughing, joking, and enjoying each other's company. In the past few months, their visits had become less and less frequent. Regardless, they still remained as close as they were when they were children. Even though the coming months would separate them by hundreds of miles, circumstances in life would bring them closer together than they had ever been.

CHAPTER VI

For the love of money is a root for all kinds of evil.
Some people, eager for money, have wandered from the
faith and pierced themselves with many griefs
Timothy 6: 10

Edward turned the car from the road, followed the drive around a small clump of trees, and parked in front of Jessie's house. He sat there for a few minutes with his head laid back against the seat, as if he had just walked to Jessie's instead of driven. It had been a hard day, and the early hours and the long work days were finally starting to take their toll on him. He thought back to Mary Alice's earlier plea for him to stay home and get some much-needed rest.

"One day I'm gonna learn to listen to that woman," he said.

He climbed from the car and followed the wooden planks that led to the barbershop at the back of the house. It wasn't really a barbershop but more of a juke joint that had been partially converted to house a beauty parlor with a separate section that served as Jessie's barbershop. There were two tables, a few chairs scattered around, and a washtub filled with ice, sodas, and beer. The entire place was as much a meeting place for Jessie and Lavern's friends as it was a beauty parlor and barbershop.

"Edward Graves," a voice called out as Edward walked in and glanced around at the all-too-familiar surroundings.

"Johnnie B.," replied Edward. "How you been? I ain't seen you in a coon's age." He pulled a chair to the table and sat down.

"Been fine," said Johnnie B. "It's good to see you. You still the hardest working man in Mississippi?"

"Working like a little slave. But it's all good. How about you, Charlie? Been a while since I seen you too," said Edward as he extended his hand to Johnnie B.'s tablemate.

"Charlie's always doing fine," interrupted Jessie as he grabbed a chair. He shook Edward's hand and sat down before Charlie could respond. "How else a man gonna be doin' when somebody sends him a check every month for nothing?"

"Man, the government still sending you them checks?" asked Edward.

"Every month," Charlie said proudly.

"You ever find out why?," asked Edward, somewhat surprised.

"Nope," said Charlie. " I don't know why and I don't care why. I don't know nuthin' about nuthin' when it comes to those checks." He said it with as much implied ignorance as possible.

"How long they been sending you them checks?" asked Edward, almost in disbelief.

"Well," started Charlie. "I guess I been getting' them for almost five years now. When I got the first one, I didn't think much about it. I thought everybody that was in the army got one, but y'all didn't say nuthin'. The next month I got another one, so I cashed that one too. Man, I was ridin' high. Then the next month I got another one. I was a little concerned about that one, so I decided not to cash it. I didn't want Mr. Richardson down at the bank to know I had that much money. But they just kept on sending me checks. Sometimes I would get two in a month, sometimes none. One month I got three. I never know when they gonna come. I got a little worried and started puttin'

45

them up. Then I started hidin' 'em. Pretty soon I had checks hid everywhere and they just kept on sending more checks."

"Man," he said drawing the word out. "I was getting scared and didn't know what to do. I thought about burning them, but then I thought, what if one day they want their money back? I couldn't sleep and all I could think about was them checks. I had to do something. Finally, I got all the checks, put them in a bag, and went to see Johnnie B. He always had money and seemed pretty smart. Plus, we all knew who he really was."

It had long been rumored that a powerful, black numbers man had been banished from Chicago and was living in Mississippi. It seemed that he had shot and killed a rival following an argument over disputed territory. Because both men exercised considerable influence in the black community, and each had such a large following, retaliation for the shooting was inevitable.

The whites, who controlled everything from gambling to the politicians, felt that the killing of the shooter would lead to an all-out war between the two sides that would affect everyone. It was decided by those in control that the shooter be exiled to Mississippi for a "cooling off period" where he would live under their protection. His territory in Chicago was divided into four parts. One-fourth would go to the whites in control as "payment for their generosity," one-fourth to the shooter's associates, one-fourth to the victim's associates, and the shooter was allowed to keep the remaining portion.

After the initial agreement was reached, the shooter was taken to Tupelo, Mississippi where he was introduced to a Mr. Thomas Montgomery. Mr. Montgomery owned the local bank, headed the local chapter of the Ku Klux Klan, and basically controlled the lives of the blacks in that region. The shooter's money would be sent to Mr. Montgomery's bank once a month. As payment for the guarantee of his safety, the shooter was to pay Mr. Montgomery ten percent of the monthly deposits. Even after the division of his territory and Mr. Montgomery's ten percent, the shooter's income was still substantial.

From the beginning, life in Mississippi proved difficult for the shooter. His attitude and behavior towards whites boarded on life-threatening. Had it not been for the pistol he was known to carry and the protection of Mr. Montgomery and his people, he would not have survived the first few months in Mississippi. Finally, tiring of the notoriety, the constant stares, and the unspoken threats, he decided to seek a more anonymous existence and moved to Starkville. Even in Starkville, stories of the man from Chicago who was protected by the whites followed him. That was the man they all came to know as "Johnnie B."

"When Charlie told me about those checks, I told him he was crazy," said Johnnie B. "If there's one thing I know about, it's money. Then he showed me a bag stuffed full of checks. When I heard the whole story, I laughed till I cried. I couldn't believe he'd saved those checks for all those years without cashing them." He stood and walked over to the tub to get the four of them a beer.

"I did cash a few," corrected Charlie with a hint of embarrassment.

"Charge these to Charlie," said Johnnie B. He handed everyone a beer, sat down, looked at Charlie, and just shook his head. "And then he had the nerve to ask me what should he do."

"Man," said Charlie, again drawing the word out. "I didn't know what to do. I didn't think black folks was allowed to have that much money."

Johnnie B. took a sip of his beer and laughed at the memory of it all. "I told him the first thing he should do was cash the checks. He couldn't do it around here, so I took him to Tupelo to see my man Mr. Montgomery. Old man Montgomery don't care where the money comes from as long as he gets his ten percent.

"When we get to the bank, I told Charlie not to say a word to anybody no matter what. I told him to act like he don't know nothing about nothing. Well, when we got to the bank, I introduced Charlie to old man Montgomery. I told him Charlie had some disability checks that he wanted to cash. I said Charlie had lost his hearing in an explosion during the war so the government sends him disability checks. I said there's no reason to talk to Charlie because he couldn't hear. So the first thing old man Montgomery did was turn to Charlie and ask him how he was doing. I thought, 'Oh Lord, Charlie gonna answer him 'cause he ain't used to ignoring white folks when they speak to him.' Charlie got a real scared look on his face and looked at me, then he looked at Mr. Montgomery, then he looked at me again as if he didn't quite know what to do. Finally, he looked down at the floor and didn't say a word.

"'Can he talk?' old man Montgomery asked me. He didn't wait for an answer. He just sat down, dumped the checks on his desk, and started adding them up. When he finished counting, he kinda smiled and got that funny look on his face that folks down here get when they think they about to get some money."

"How much did he have?" asked Edward. He leaned back and tried to visualize Mr. Montgomery's expression.

"He had a good little piece of money," said Johnnie B., impressed with Charlie's frugality. "He had twenty-six checks for eight hundred and twenty-six dollars apiece, a little over twenty-one thousand dollars."

"And he didn't know what to do?" asked Edward in amazement. "A black man in Mississippi with that much money, and he didn't know what to do."

"What would you have did?" asked Charlie as if he still wasn't quite sure what to do.

"Left Mississippi," answered Jessie and Edward in unison. They slapped hands and had a hearty laugh at Charlie's expense.

"I ain't going nowhere as long as they keep sending me them checks," said Charlie as if that was the one thing he was sure of.

"So what did you do?" asked Edward. He wondered why he had never heard the story before.

"Well," answered Johnnie B. for Charlie, as if Charlie really couldn't hear. Old man Montgomery figured something wasn't quite right. So, he decided as a favor to me he would cash the checks, keep the money in his bank, and charge Charlie ten percent."

"So," added Charlie, "every now and then, me and Johnnie B. take us a ride to Tupelo and get us some money, old man Montgomery gets paid, and everybody's happy."

"Everybody?" asked Johnnie B. as if he didn't quite understand the word. "Everybody ain't happy. Old man Montgomery's happy, you shouldn't be, and I ain't." He looked at Charlie, sipped his beer, and tried to find the right words to explain what he meant.

Johnnie B had learned a long time ago that blacks and the whites in power viewed money differently. Over the years as his fortunes grew, his attitude about money became more and more like that of the whites who created the imbalanced system under which he lived. They system dictated that money was simply a tool to be used for what it could do and not what it could buy. Money made money. Material things would come. Johnnie B. had refined that philosophy to a fine art and had enjoyed the power, control, and freedom his money had provided. Even in Mississippi he lived by that philosophy. His payments to the people in Chicago and to Mr. Montgomery were what basically kept him alive.

He looked at Charlie who had enough money to enjoy some of life's freedoms and wondered what had happened to his people in Mississippi. *Sitting in Mississippi waiting on a check ain't living, and it sure won't bring happiness.* He sipped his beer and leaned back in his chair, wondering why he was even in Mississippi. But he knew why and he was not happy.

"I know why old man Montgomery is happy and I know why I ain't, but what you got to be so happy about?" asked Johnnie B. He sipped the last of his beer and tossed the empty can in the trash.

"Why shouldn't I be?" asked Charlie. He walked over to the tub to get Johnnie B. another beer. "I got money in the bank and checks coming in. Tell me life ain't good. Here, this one's on me too." He handed Johnnie B another beer and sat down. Charlie sensed a slight irritation in Johnnie B.'s voice and expression. He decided to be less humorous and a little more serious. He knew Johnnie B. was not one to be trifled with.

"Look," said Charlie. "I ain't foolin' myself into thinkin' I'm smart 'cause I got a little money, lucky maybe, but not smart. What I do know is that no matter how much money a black man got, he cain't be happy in Mississippi. The only thing I got to be happy about is that somebody somewhere made a mistake about something. You think I'm happy sitting here in Mississippi waiting on somebody to send me a check? That ain't livin', but I cain't leave, not as long as they keep sending me money. It's like I'm being paid to stay here."

"What if they don't stop sending you checks?" asked Jessie. "You gonna just sit here waiting on checks forever?"

"I don't know," answered Charlie. "I just don't know."

"One day somebody's going to correct that mistake and them checks going to stop coming," said Edward.

"You think so?" asked Charlie, as if that would be the answer to his nonexistent problem. "If the checks stop I'll probably come to Ohio where y'all going to be."

"Ohio? When you going to Ohio?" asked Johnnie B. "What part you going to?"

"Leaving in the spring for a place called Akron," answered Jessie. "You ever been there?"

"Nope. Been to Cleveland," answered Johnnie B. "Akron ain't too far from there. They got a lot of factories. Is that what you plan on doing, working in the factory?"

"For a while," answered Jessie. "Then I'm going to open up a barbershop with a beauty parlor attached to it like this one," he said proudly.

Johnnie B. looked around at the sparsely furnished room and they all laughed.

"Maybe not exactly like this one," said Jessie. He had to laugh too at the thought of a barbershop in Akron looking like this one in Mississippi.

"What about you?" asked Johnnie B., turning his attention to Edward.

"I'll get a job until I get enough money to open me a real nice restaurant and sell lots of barbecue" answered Edward. "You know, that's all I ever done is cook. Even in the army I was a cook. All those black folks with factory jobs got to eat. You know white folks don't know how to cook for 'em. That's where I come in."

"What about your horses?" asked Johnnie B. "You can't take horses to Ohio with you."

It was a well-known fact that Edward raised some of the finest horses in the county. If Johnnie B. could just buy a few, they would be prized possessions for him.

"I'm selling Sam a few head and he'll look after the rest for me. It ain't like I'm leaving for good. I was born in Mississippi, and I've got too much not to come back now and then," he said. "I'll be back."

"You want to sell me a couple?" asked Johnnie B., almost reluctantly.

Edward thought for a moment before answering. "Sure," he finally said. "I got a couple of real good ones I'll let you look at."

"Thanks," said Johnnie B., genuinely appreciative of the offer. "Now, let me do something for you. Things are going to be different for you up North, and there's two things you're going to need. You're going to need some money, and you're going to need a white man with some power who's willing to help you get ahead. I'm going to give you both of 'em. 'Course, you'll have to share the white man, but that shouldn't be a problem."

Charlie leaned forward, listening intently to every word Johnnie B. said. How could he possibly give them a white man? Would he give them one to take with them, or would he have one waiting for them in Ohio? Charlie didn't understand at all.

Johnnie B. noticed not only Charlie's interest but Edward's and Jessie's as well. He hesitated long enough to make sure that he had their undivided attention before continuing. "In about a month I'll be going back to Tupelo to see old man Montgomery. I'm going to have him send some money to a bank in Akron and open an account in your names. I'll get the name of the man in charge at the bank and have Montgomery send some money to him for his personal use. That's going to be your white man.

"Every month I'll have Montgomery send your man some money as payment to give you whatever you need. It can be a loan for your business, a loan for a house, a car, anything. If you have any trouble, I'll pay your man a little more money. If that don't work, I'll have old man Montgomery send some of his people up there to straighten things out. Either way, it shouldn't be a problem. You'd be surprised what you can get done with a little money," said Johnnie B., looking directly at Charlie.

"Now remember." he continued. "Don't be like most folks and just walk into the bank looking for somebody to help you.

You gonna have a man. Ask for him, because you'll be there on business not to cash a check," he said, still looking at Charlie.

Johnnie B. paused, sipped his beer, and hoped Edward and Jessie understood what he was trying to do. Johnnie B. was a good man. Though he could pose a danger if threatened, for a friend there was no limit to what he would do. Edward, Jessie, and Charlie were his friends.

"Why you doing this for us?" asked Edward.

"Because you're my friends," answered Johnnie B. with no hesitation or further explanation.

"We all got plenty of friends" said Jessie.

"I don't," said Johnnie B., almost with regret. "I only got a few."

Charlie sat wide-eyed staring at Johnnie B, totally fascinated by all that he had just heard. Was it possible that Johnnie B. could do all he said? And if so, why was a man like him even in Mississippi? "Why don't you leave here?" he finally asked. "You don't belong in Mississippi."

Just as Johnnie B. was about to answer, Edward interrupted. "Charlie's right. You don't belong in Mississippi. If you stay here long enough, white folks gonna get tired of you and hang you and do you just like they did that Till boy over in Money."

"He was from Chicago just like you," added Jessie.

Johnnie B. smiled. "They might hang my body, but they ain't gonna hang Johnnie B." He patted his pocket with the ever-present pistol. He smiled, but deep down inside he knew that if he stayed in Mississippi he would die in Mississippi. His life was in constant danger, not only from whites who were unaware of Mr. Montgomery's protective order, but from envious blacks who were equally unaware. If he returned to Chicago a similar fate awaited him.

Johnnie B. looked around the table at the few friends he had left. Somewhere along the way he had made a wrong turn. Now, he thought, if he could just do something to help his friends, maybe that would get him back on the right track. He reached into his pocket and pulled out a pencil and a small pad of paper. He wrote a phone number on it and handed it to Charlie.

"Take this," he said. "If anything ever happens to me, call this number in Chicago. Ask for Mildred and explain to her what happened. She'll know what to do."

"Who's Mildred?" asked Charlie.

"She's the one who got me started in the business. She's a little older, so show some respect and listen to what she says. You'll learn a few things."

"Does she know about old man Montgomery?" asked Charlie. He realized that without Johnnie B., he would need somebody to talk to Mr. Montgomery for him.

"Yup," answered Johnnie B. "She knows the whole story and would just love to meet you. Every time I talk to her, she asks about you and laughs about those checks. She'll make sure you get your money up in Tupelo. You just make sure you call her."

Charlie folded the paper and tucked it inside his wallet for safekeeping. "Thanks man." he said. He leaned back in his chair and stretched.

It was getting late and Charlie decided to get the haircut he had come for. Edward decided his could wait; there was still a birthday cake to be delivered. Johnnie B. had business to attend to, but there was always time for one last beer with his friends.

"Fellas, I gotta go," said Edward. He stood and shook hands all around. "Today's David's birthday and I still got the cake in the car. His momma gonna kill me if I don't get home with it soon. Jessie, I'll get that haircut tomorrow. Charlie, take care of yourself, and Johnnie B., thanks, man." He shook Johnnie B.'s hand again, turned, and walked out the door.

That was the last time Edward saw Johnnie B. Johnnie B. didn't get the chance to give Jessie and Edward their white man or open the bank account he had promised. He was killed less than a month later near Greenwood. Three men, unaware of who Johnnie B. really was, attempted to rob him following a card game. Two of the robbers and Johnnie B. were killed during the attempt.

Word of his death spread quickly through Mississippi and soon reached Starkville, then Tupelo and finally Mr. Montgomery. Mr. Montgomery sent a small group of men to hunt down the surviving robber and issue the appropriate warning and punishment. Johnnie B. was not to have been harmed in any way by anyone. Being unaware of that order was no excuse.

One week after Johnnie B.'s death, the surviving robber was located and he was hanged. His lifeless body was found hanging from a tree directly in front of the house in which Johnnie B. was killed. It was rumored that from that day forth, because of the violation of the protective order, any relative or associate of Johnnie B. who came to Mississippi would be under that same protection. Any violation of that protective order by anyone meant certain death by hanging from that very same tree. That order still applies to this day.

When word of Johnnie B.'s death reach Charlie, he did as he had been instructed. He called Mildred and explained what had happened. The next day, after saying his good-byes to Edward and Jessie, Charlie left Mississippi for Chicago.

CHAPTER VII

This one thing I do, forgetting those things which are behind and reaching forth unto those things which are before.

Philippians 3: 12

Fall, then winter, slipped away and spring returned to Mississippi with its usual warm, wet weather, an abundance of magnolias, and a promise of prosperity. Edward had sold the restaurant for more than expected, and he and Mary Alice had finally found a renter for their place. Even without Johnnie B.'s help there was enough money to get them to Ohio and carry them through the first year. With a job and a little luck it wouldn't take long to open their restaurant once they reached Ohio. Times weren't good, just not as bad. Sam loved to tell them that God was smiling on them and all was as it should be. Mary Alice chose to believe Sam.

Even so, as the day of departure drew near, there was a nervous sense of near-uneasiness about Mary Alice. Some of it could be attributed to the trip itself, but for the most part it was simply a mother's concern. To take her children and all that she owned to an unfamiliar place such a long way from home would test the mettle of any mother. For Mary Alice, even though this was what she had waited so long for, it was still very difficult.

Edward understood her feelings but did not realize the depth of them, so the comfort he tried to provide was not enough to give the support she needed. It was a very delicate time for Mary Alice, and she constantly prayed for God to give her strength. God heard her prayers, but it was still difficult. In addition, not knowing what awaited them in Ohio only added to the difficulty.

Had it not been for the letters she received from Sophie, she would have had no idea what to expect once she left Mississippi. The first letter was one of those quick "hello I'll get back to you later" kind of letters. However, it did provide Mary Alice with an address and some sense of comfort knowing that her friend in Ohio had not forgotten her. Minnie and Lavern also received one of those same letters. They all answered immediately, each of them eager to give Sophie the latest news from home.

The next letters were more in line with what Mary Alice had hoped for. They provided answers to most of her questions and eased some of her concerns. Now, with some idea of what to expect, her confidence was once again high. She was better able to deal with her motherly concerns. It would be a few more days before they left, but the time to leave was almost at hand.

The children were finally showing the excitement Mary Alice had hoped for, and they were spending their last few days "saying good-bye to the horses." Edward, with no crops to plant or restaurant to attend to, was spending his last few days in Mississippi being the gentleman of leisure Mary Alice always wanted him to be. Even though he knew it was only temporary, he enjoyed the feeling and took the time to get some much-needed rest.

Mary Alice was finally at peace with herself. The indecision, the guilt, and the fear were all gone. Sam was right; all was as it should be she thought. She leaned back in her chair, closed her eyes, and enjoyed the peace that had so long eluded her. She had no idea that in the midst of her peace the storm of life was forming. It would be a storm of such magnitude that only God could explain it. It would change their lives forever.

She opened her eyes momentarily and caught a glimpse of Edward, the man God had so graciously placed in her life. He was in the driveway with Sam and Jessie as the three of them changed a tire on his car. *How many men does it take to change a tire,* she wondered. She smiled as she answered her own question. *It must take three.*

"Girl, what you sitting there smiling about" asked Lavern.

"You ain't heard a word we said," added Minnie. "You sitting there like you lost in space."

Mary Alice didn't answer or even pretend she had been listening to their conversation. She just closed her eyes again and continued to enjoy her newfound serenity. It wasn't long before her thoughts drifted back to Edward. She thought about the difference he had made in her life and the joy he brought to it. She smiled again as she thought about that night on the porch when he finally said it was time to leave Mississippi. She remembered sitting there holding his hand, unsure of what the future held, but confident that as long as they faced it together their lives would be fine. To Mary Alice, it was if God had willed it. She shifted in her chair and said a silent prayer of thanks because God had been good to her and she knew it.

In the background she could hear Sam and Jessie discussing the merits of a Hudson and the soft laughter of Minnie and Lavern as they read one of Sophie's letters. She listened as they joked about Sophie's description of the projects and the snow.

Footsteps on the porch caught her attention. She thought of a snowman, and this time she not only smiled, but laughed. She looked up to see Edward standing in front of her.

"Hey you," he said as he leaned down and kissed her softly on the lips.

"Hey you," she answered as she returned the kiss along with a light hug. "I was just sitting here thinking about you," she added.

"So that's what you was sitting there smiling and laughing about?" joked Lavern.

"Mind your own business," said Mary Alice, laughing as she spoke.

"Amen," said Minnie.

"Come on," said Mary Alice, taking Edward's hand. "Sit down right here. We need to get a man's point of view on some things."

"No problem. Ain't too often I get the chance to enjoy the company of so many lovely ladies," said Edward. He pulled a chair next to Mary Alice and sat down. *Always the perfect gentleman,* she thought as she leaned her head against his shoulder.

"Now, what is it you need to know?" he asked.

"I need to know about the snow in Ohio," said Mary Alice, laughing but genuinely curious about the weather in Ohio.

"Girl, you gonna see snow soon enough," said Lavern. "What we need to know about are the people in Ohio, especially the white people."

"What about them?" asked Edward. "You know how white folks are."

"You know what she means," said Mary Alice as she raised her head from Edward's shoulder, not at all satisfied with the generality of his answer.

"You sound like Sophie," added Minnie. "She always saying the same thing about being black and knowing how white folks are."

Edward smiled, somewhat surprised by their sudden seriousness. He looked from Lavern to Minnie, then at Sam and Jessie walking toward the porch.

"Ask Sam," he said. "See what he got to say."

"Why should we think Sam knows anymore about white folks in Ohio than you already told us?" asked Lavern.

"Which is nothing," added Minnie.

"Ain't that the truth," said Mary Alice.

"Because he's Sam," answered Edward as if no further explanation was needed.

His name was Samuel Walter Ellison, and when it came to the stereotypical Southern black man, he was the exception to the rule. Like Johnnie B., intelligent and unafraid, he had a clear understanding of the workings of the political, social, and financial systems under which they all lived. He did not suffer from the lack of confidence and the attitude of inferiority that a history of slavery had instilled in most black people in the South.

Unlike most black people who traced their ancestry back to Africa through slavery, Sam's ancestors left Africa as free people in order to escape the slave traders and maintain their freedom. They left Africa and traveled north, along the coast of Morocco into Spain. They settled there temporarily before crossing the Pyrenees Mountains into France. In France they found safe haven and settled outside of Paris in the town of Orleans. There they found employment under the tutelage of a local textile company owner.

Over the years the company grew. When it expanded its business to Louisiana in America, Sam's grandfather adopted the last name of his employer and moved to America. After generations of the family working for the company in France and in America, Sam's father took his savings and left the company. He moved his family to Starkville, Mississippi where he purchased the farm Sam now owned.

"Hey man," said Edward, addressing both Sam and Jessie as they approached the porch. "The ladies want to know about the white people in Ohio."

"What about them?" asked Sam. He grabbed the support pole and pulled himself up onto the porch. "You know how white folks are."

Jessie mumbled something in agreement and sat down on the steps.

"So, what're you saying?" asked Lavern, now less amused and slightly irritated by the lack of a satisfactory answer. "You telling me that white folks in Ohio gonna be just like the ones in Mississippi and there's no difference?"

Jessie nodded, more amused at his wife's irritation than he was interested in answering her question.

"Well," she said, now more than slightly irritated. "If that's what you telling me, I ain't gonna put up with it, and I mean it. When I leave Mississippi, there's some things I plan on leaving in Mississippi. I ain't gonna travel all the way to Ohio and have to put up with the same foolishness I have to put up with in Mississippi, and I mean it. You can laugh if you want to," she said, glaring at Jessie, her attitude just short of being hostile.

"Lavern's right," said Mary Alice, sitting up in her chair and nudging Edward. "Why we want to go such a long ways from home and nothing's going to change?"

"Listen," said Sam. He stood there, slowly shaking his head as he listened to Mary Alice and Lavern. He raised his hat and wiped the sweat from his forehead. "Where you think you goin'? You ain't leaving the country, you just leaving Mississippi." He removed his hat, turned, and faced the ladies. He stood there silently, hat in hand, looking directly at Lavern. "Look at me," he said. "Tell me what you see."

Lavern glanced at Mary Alice and Minnie as if waiting for them to answer Sam's question for her. Getting no response from either of her friends, she leaned back in her chair, folded her arms across her chest, and looked up at Sam.

"What do you see?" he repeated. He looked deep into her eyes as if searching for the answer to his own question.

"I see Minnie's husband," said Mary Alice. She and Minnie laughed as if her unsolicited answer was the punch line to their own private joke.

Lavern didn't laugh. She simply leaned forward in her chair and returned Sam's gaze, intrigued by the question, not quite knowing how to answer it. What did she see? What did they see, she wondered. What did white folks see? What did Mr. Richardson down at the bank see when Sam made his deposits? What did she see? She looked closer, silently staring, wondering what should she see. What did Sam see when he looked in the mirror?

Finally she saw. She saw what they all saw. She saw what white folks saw. She saw what Mr. Richardson down at the bank saw when Sam made his deposits. She saw what Sam saw when he looked in the mirror. She saw a black man. She saw a black man when she knew she should have just seen a man. She leaned back in her chair, crossed her legs, and smiled at the complexity of the question and the simplicity of the answer.

Sam noticed the change in her expression. He placed his hat back on his head and leaned back against the support pole. Before Lavern could speak, he answered for her. "You see a black man." He said it slowly and softly, almost in a whisper, as if it were a painful truth. He paused to let the words sink in, to make sure they all heard him before he continued. "White folks in Mississippi and white folks in Ohio see the same thing. There's no difference in them. The difference is going to have to be in you."

"What do you mean?" asked Lavern. She had been far too long in Mississippi to have any idea what Sam meant. Mary Alice leaned her head back against Edward's shoulder, equally unsure what Sam meant. But like Lavern, she wanted to hear an explanation.

"Let me put it this way," said Sam. "In Mississippi you don't want white folks to know too much about you. You really don't even want them to know who you are," he said with a slight smile. "It can be dangerous down here when they start knowing you by name. Oh, a few of them might recognize you, nod and call you 'boy' or 'gal,' but that's exactly what you want. It's safer that way," he added.

They knew he was right. They all knew there was a certain sense of safety in Mississippi in being anonymous. Sam looked around for a chair, a stool, or something else to sit on, but decided against it and continued to lean against the support pole.

"You two really gotta be different," he said to Jessie and Edward a little louder than he meant to. Jessie jumped as if surprised he was being spoken to. Edward and Sam both laughed at his reaction.

"First thing you both gotta do in Ohio is let them know you ain't nobody's boy," said Sam. "Let them know you a black man with a name and you expect to be called by that name." This time when he said "black man," he said it proudly and emphatically, as though it were more of a proclamation than a mere statement of fact. "If you don't let them know, they're gonna treat you just like they treat you down here, like somebody's boy."

"You sound just like Johnnie B.," said Jessie.

"Yeah, whatever," answered Sam. "More black folks need to sound like Johnnie B. and act like him too. When it came to white folks and money, Johnnie B knew what he was talking about."

"Yeah, and you see what happened to him," said Edward.

"Well, white folks didn't kill him," answered Sam.

"They would have," said Jessie.

"No they wouldn't," said Sam. "They was scared of him. Plus, he had money and they was getting some. You know how people get about money, black and white. But then he gets killed by some black folks who don't know no better. That's the tragedy of it all. Sometimes we can be our own worst enemy, and that's especially true up North in places like Ohio. So y'all be careful. I mean it. Be careful."

"Johnnie B. use to say the same thing about Chicago," said Jessie.

"Well, you pretend it's Chicago and be careful," said Sam.

They knew what he meant. It was the ladies who needed reminding. He looked at Mary Alice and Lavern. Mary Alice sat with her head laid against Edward's shoulder, a look of satisfied curiosity on her face as if she understood and needed to hear every word Sam had to say. Lavern sat motionless, expressionless, silent, thinking about all she had just heard.

"Are things ever gonna change?" she asked. She said it almost in a whisper, a hint of sadness in her voice, speaking to no one in particular but to anyone who would answer. For what seemed like the longest time, no one answered. Her husband looked around uneasily.

"Ain't nothing gonna change down here," Jessie finally said. "It's like the world's forgotten about black folks in Mississippi."

They all looked at Jessie. Edward nodded in agreement while Sam reacted as if that was the most absurd thing he had ever heard.

"Oh, it's going to change," said Sam. He said it strongly, boldly, confidently, defiantly. He said it as if things better change or the powers that be would have to deal with him personally. He said it as if he were ready at that very moment to stand up, march straight to the capital building, kick open the door, and shout, "Enough!" " It's going to change."

"What?" asked Jessie. "You gonna change Mississippi? "You just like Johnnie B., you shouldn't even be in Mississippi. You need to come on with us to Ohio and leave this madness. You ain't going to do nothing down here but get yourself in trouble."

"I might cause some trouble," answered Sam, again with a sense of defiance. "I figure somebody's got to stay here and make white folks understand that what they're doing to us is wrong. Otherwise, they're gonna always think it's right. You know how white folks down here can be."

"I know how they can be and I know how you can get," said Jessie. "So you be careful."

"Jessie's right," said Mary Alice. 'You be careful."

Mary Alice stood and walked to the edge of the porch to look for her kids. *Those kids should be back by now,* she thought. It was getting late and there was still a host of things remaining to be done—mostly clothes and dishes to pack. They weren't taking much but they were taking all they had.

Movement near the barn caught her attention, and she leaned against the other support pole and watched the kids as they unsaddled the mare before leading her to the enclosure near the rear of the house. Satisfied that the kids and the horse were all safe, Mary Alice returned to her chair and once again laid her head on Edward's shoulder.

Lavern stood and patted Mary Alice on the head. "Get some rest," she said. She walked over and grabbed Jessie by the arm to lift him up from the steps. "It's getting late. We still have to get the kids from Momma's."

Instead of standing, Jessie pulled Lavern down until she was sitting on the step next to him. "In a minute" he said. "Them kids going to be fine."

"Y'all don't have to hurry," said Edward. "Sam, Minnie, how about it? I got some beer in the cooler out in the barn."

"Yeah," said Mary Alice, finally sitting up in her chair. "Don't rush off. I'll make us some coffee and see if I can fix up a little something to eat for everybody." She stood and headed for the door. There was always food for company.

"Let me help," said Minnie as she and Lavern both followed Mary Alice inside.

"Guess I'll get the beer," said Edward.

"Sounds good to me," encouraged Sam.

And so it went, late into the night. Good friends, good food, a few cold beers, and some hot coffee to help the ladies fight off the evening chill. Sam and Minnie would miss their friends, but tonight was not the time for the sadness of farewells. It was a time for prayer and thanks. They prayed that God would protect the ones leaving Mississippi for a place such a long ways from home. They gave thanks for their friendship. They gave thanks because God had been good to them and they knew it.

Two days later, at a little after two o'clock in the morning, Edward and Jessie packed their families and all their belongings into their cars. There were still places in Alabama and Tennessee that were best traveled during daylight hours. After one final prayer, they left Mississippi for Ohio, the women and children with the confidence they would get there, and the men with the concern they would get them there safely.

Chapter VIII

For he will command his angels concerning you to guard
you in all your ways; they will lift you up in their hands,
so that you will not strike your foot against a stone.
Psalm 91:11,12

Twenty-two hours was a long time to drive a car. As a matter of fact, twenty-two hours was a long time to be in a car. So what started out as simply a long drive quickly turned into a journey. It was a journey of hundreds and hundreds of miles. A journey that encompassed five states and far too many deeply segregated Southern towns with signs that proudly proclaimed their racism. Towns with signs that read "white only" or "Impeach Thurgood Marshall." Some signs simply said "colored."

"Who is Thurgood Marshall?" asked David more times than Mary Alice cared to count.

"What's impeach and why they want to do that to him?" asked Doug.

They just didn't understand. It had been question after question after question, and they never did receive what they considered satisfactory answers.

The journey took them from Mississippi into Alabama, up through Tuscaloosa, then into Birmingham. At that point, Edward had left the confines of familiar territory, and from there on it would be a new experience for them all. Ahead lay the long stretch North through Tennessee before they reached Kentucky and the Ohio River which separates Kentucky from Ohio. Once they crossed the river, it would only be a few more hours until they reached Akron and their new home. So they pushed on.

Just before midnight they arrived in Akron. Edward found a telephone and called Johnathan for their pre-arranged place to stay. Johnathan and Sophie were expecting them. They knew it was going to be a full house, but with the right combination of pillows and blankets strategically placed, there was room for all. The three families would stay together until Jessie and Edward moved their families into apartments in the projects located within walking distance of Johnathan and Sophie's house.

When Sophie first arrived in Akron, she and Johnathan saw the projects for what they really were: temporary Government Housing Projects, or projects for short. Sophie understood temporary, and they bought a house as soon as they got jobs. She hoped Mary Alice and Lavern would do the same.

For Lavern and Mary Alice, their first impression of the projects was one of curiosity, then disappointment, and finally acceptance. Their apartment was located in a building containing four separate apartments, each unit having the same basic design. Mary Alice's apartment was next door to Lavern's. Whether it was arranged or purely coincidental, Mary Alice was truly grateful. Each unit had one door that offered one way in and one way out. That was not their idea of safety or sensible planning. There were no interior doors connecting the apartments. Most units in the other buildings did have a front and a back door.

From the moment Mary Alice entered her apartment she felt almost claustrophobic. To the right of the only door was a small kitchen—a very small kitchen. Against the wall in the living area was the only source of heat, a small gas heater. Off to each side of the living area was a bedroom. Each appeared only slightly larger than the kitchen. Near the bedroom on the right was a bathroom with no bathtub but with a shower. Mary Alice had expected indoor plumbing but it was still a relief to actually see it.

So, this is going to be home, she thought. She stood on the sidewalk outside of her apartment waiting on Lavern. She gazed out over the seemingly endless sea of apartment buildings.

"Lot of buildings, ain't it?" said Lavern. She stepped out of her apartment, closed the door, and double checked the lock. "I just love these sidewalks." She clicked her heels against the sidewalk as she walked, enjoying the sound. It was so different from that of gravel and dirt roads. "I think I'm going to like it here," she said as she surveyed their new surroundings.

"So many buildings," said Mary Alice. "I ain't never seen nothing like it. The streets, the sidewalks everywhere, and all the cars and people."

"Don't worry, you'll get use to it" said Lavern, amused at her young friends innocence. Come on, let's get the kids and go. I told Jessie we would be at Sophie's an hour ago" said Lavern. Even in Ohio she was living up to her nickname of "Late Freight." "He could have at least left me the car and rode with Edward. Your car just sitting here and they know you don't drive. Telling me I don't know my way around Akron yet. Neither do they."

It was a short walk to Sophie's house and the weather was nice, though not quite as warm as they were accustomed to for this time of year. It was a little overcast but still a nice day for a walk, and the kids were eager to go.

"Stay on the sidewalk and slow down," shouted Lavern. The four kids left the little playground area and raced to see who could reach the sidewalk first. The kids loved the sidewalk as much as Lavern. They knew that if they followed it as it weaved its way through the projects, it would eventually exit onto a main street. From there, it was simply take a right turn at the stop sign, go two blocks, take another right turn, and Sophie lived in the second house. For the kids, the walk to Sophie's was an adventure in itself. They always looked forward to it, plus the fact that they all loved Sophie.

"Why they got streetlights over the sidewalk?" asked David. He tossed a rock at the lamp before realizing that his mother was following and probably watching him.

"It's to keep the monster away when he comes out at night," answered Doug. "You're safe as long as you stay on the sidewalk and the streetlights are on."

"Monster?" asked Julie and they all stopped. "Monster?" she asked again, not quite sure what he meant but fearful of the implication. At five years old, the mere mention of a monster was almost more than her little brother Alfred could stand. He was tempted to run back to his mother and Mary Alice but he held his ground.

Doug continued to walk and the other kids quickly followed. Alfred was still uneasy about the monster and occasionally glanced back at his mother. Julie, at seven years old, felt that she had to at least be braver than a five-year-old and six-year-old boy. She playfully pushed Doug in the back and with as much confidence as possible said, "There ain't no such thing as a monster."

"Yes it is," said Doug. "Ask David. He knows. He saw it."

David, who had been unusually quiet remained that way. He did not want to discuss anything at all about the monster. As for little Alfred, that was the last thing he wanted to hear, that they had actually seen it. He stopped dead in his tracks, and it was becoming more and more difficult for him to hold his ground and not retreat backwards to the safety of his mother.

"You actually saw it?" asked Julie. She was still doubtful of the existence of a monster, but her doubt was fading fast. Alfred stopped again and this time he actually took a small step backwards before reluctantly continuing on with the others.

"What is wrong with those kids?" asked Lavern. She was totally unaware of her young son's dilemma but noticed his erratic behavior.

"Girl, who knows? Pay them kids no attention," answered Mary Alice. "Listen, did you know that Deacon Harvey and his wife Ethel Lee are here?"

"You can't be serious," answered Lavern "They too old to leave Mississippi."

"Ain't nobody too old to leave Mississippi," said Mary Alice.

"Well, they're too old. They was old when we were little, so you know they're too old now. What in the world are they doing up here anyway" she asked.

"They got two sons here and the kids wanted them to leave Mississippi," said Mary Alice. "I saw them the other morning when I was walking. Ethel Lee said they been here about two months. They stay in that building right over there in the end apartment. Remember Charlie from back home?"

"Tall Charlie?" asked Lavern. "The one who use to be with Johnnie B. all the time?"

"Yup, that's the one. He's here too," said Mary Alice.

"Well, if he's here, you can bet Jessie and Edward found him by now," said Lavern, still enjoying the sound of the clicking of her heels on the sidewalk.

The sky was beginning to clear and the midday sun provided an afternoon warmth almost reminiscent of Mississippi.

"The sun sure feels good," said Mary Alice. She removed her sweater and folded it across her arm, enjoying the warm breeze and the freshness of her new surroundings. It had only taken her a short time to get acquainted with her new home and to convince herself that this is where she should be. Sophie had introduced her to everyone from the iceman to the mailman, who was named

Mitch. From the corner grocery store owner named Mr. Curry, to the school crossing guard named Flora, she had met them all. They all loved and respected Sophie.

"I think I'm going to like it here," said Mary Alice.

As for the kids, the projects had been a pleasant surprise, but now with the threat of a monster looming over them, they weren't so sure.

"You actually saw it, both of you?" asked Julie. She was beginning to feel a little uneasy but was trying her best to appear brave.

"We saw his shadow one night, but that was in Mississippi" answered David. "Anyway, how does it know we're in Ohio?" He was starting to realize that it was daylight, he was in Ohio, and for now he was safe. Anyway, how could it know they were in Ohio? He knew there should be hundreds of miles between him and the thing he believed lived down by the pond on the farm in Mississippi at night.

"I don't know how it knows, but I thought I saw it the first night we was here," answered Doug.

"I don't believe you," said Julie. She was still somewhat skeptical, but nervous nonetheless.

"Me neither," said Alfred. At this point he was ready to agree with anyone who didn't believe in the monster.

"Where did you see it?" asked David.

"It was in the bushes by our window. I know it was there because the bushes kept moving and it sounded like it was pushing against the screen."

"You should say your prayers every night and ask God to send an angel to protect you," said Julie. She was now starting to display more faith and less fear.

"Did you tell your mom and dad?" asked Alfred. He was sure that prayer along with parents should be enough to save anybody from anything.

"Nope," said Doug. "Grown-ups don't believe in monsters."

"Or angels," added Julie.

"I believe in angels," said Doug. "But if God's got angels, then the Devil's got something, and I saw something down by the pond in Mississippi and something outside my window when we first got here."

"Well," said Julie. "You better start believing more in God's angels than you do in the Devil's something, 'cause if you don't, the sidewalks won't keep you safe. One night that something's gonna bust into your apartment and drag you off screaming into the dark. And you better say your prayers every night too," she said, turning her attention to David. "Or the same thing's gonna happen to you."

"I say my prayers every night," said David. He now wished he had never thrown that rock and this whole subject had never come up.

Alfred didn't have to be told to say his prayers. If that's what was required of him to be safe from the something, he was willing to stop, kneel down, and say his prayers right there on the sidewalk. Instead he reached out and grabbed his sister's hand. It was a search for security more than a show of sibling affection. He held on tightly as they continued to walk. In the distance he could see the stop sign and the street leading to Sophie's house. Soon this whole monster thing would be left behind, he thought. He quickened his steps, let go of his sister's hand, then ran towards the street and the distant stop sign. David immediately started running and screaming, thinking something must be chasing Alfred. Soon all four kids were running and laughing with all thoughts of the monster left behind as they headed towards Sophie's.

By the time Mary Alice and Lavern arrived at Sophie's, the kids had been there and gone. Sophie had given each of them a dime and, along with John, Jr., they were on their way to the corner store, which was usually the last stop on their little adventure.

"Where's my dime?" asked Mary Alice.

"You better get a job," said Sophie as if she were a mother talking to her child. They all laughed and walked up onto the porch and sat down. They still loved sitting on the porch, and Sophie had even provided a rocking chair with a fluffy cushion for some lucky guest. This time, Mary Alice chose to be the lucky one.

"You know, you're right," said Mary Alice. I do need a job." She fidgeted with her sweater before finally laying it across the back of her chair.

"Listen," said Sophie. "Jobs are easy to get up here. A lady named Grace at Bible study told me about two jobs right after we got here. One was at a rubber shop and the other one was at the telephone company. I figured what's easier than talking, so I went to the telephone company and they hired me."

"Just like that?" asked Mary Alice.

"Just like that," answered Sophie.

"I thought all those telephone operators were white. You as dark as I am," said Mary Alice, surprised almost to the point of disbelief.

"Nope, they just sound that way," said Sophie. "Look, the first thing you gotta do up here is learn to speak the King's English. You a black woman, so you gotta learn to sound like the queen when you speak. Girl, you should hear me at work. I sound like the queen herself. Then they just look at me like they don't understand. It's like I'm speaking some foreign language, a black woman sounding white.

"So that's what I got to learn to do, speak proper if I want to get a job?" asked Mary Alice. She really didn't understand the necessity of being nearly bilingual.

"Yep, it's easy. First we're going to see about getting you a home church then back to school," said Sophie.

"The church is always a good place to start," said Mary Alice.

"Amen," said Lavern.

"And what about you, Miss Amen? You want to lose that Mississippi accent?" asked Sophie.

"No thank you, ma'am," answered Lavern. "I'll just go with what I got, thank you. You need to teach her to drive while you at it."

"You ain't learn to drive yet?" asked Sophie. "Girl, everybody up here, even most of the kids, can drive a car. We cain't let you be the only grown woman in the projects who can't drive a car."

"She was the only one in Mississippi," said Lavern.

"No, I wasn't. Katie up in West Point couldn't drive, either," said Mary Alice. "Anyways, I'll be driving before you know it." She removed her sweater from the back of her chair and wrapped it around her shoulders. The shade from the porch had stolen some of the sun's warmth and her sweater provided a convenient substitute. She crossed her legs and leaned back in her chair, enjoying the slow, easy rocking motion. A slight breeze blew across the porch but the sweater served its purpose.

In the distance she could see the children returning from the store, running and laughing, as happy as ever. The adjustment to their new home had been easier than Mary Alice had hoped. It seemed happiness had followed them from Ohio to Mississippi.

As for Edward, things couldn't have been better. From the time he arrived in Ohio, he could sense a presence, a being, a spirit or something watching over him and assuring him that everything would be all right. At times the sensation was so strong that he wanted to speak to it. The only reason he didn't was because he didn't know what to say or who to say it to, so he kept it to himself. Even though the feeling was almost supernatural, it felt good.

Mary Alice felt the same thing, but it was something she had felt since she was a child. Her mother told her it was because she was blessed and had God's favor. What she felt was an angel that would always be with her. "If you're ever in need, if you ever lose your way and feel that life has gotten the best of you, call your angel," her mother said. Little did Mary Alice know how desperately her angel would soon be needed, and how devastating the reasons for that need would be to them all.

But for now, all was as it should be. Mary Alice stopped rocking her chair, leaned back, raised her arms, and stretched in full appreciation of all that God had provided. She had good friends, a wonderful family, and this glorious day. She said thanks, almost out loud, because God had been good to her and she knew it.

CHAPTER IX

As ye have received Christ Jesus the Lord so walk ye in him. Colossians 1:6

Akron was a long ways from Mississippi, both geographically and socially, so the transition from one to the other was rather difficult for some. For Charlie, the difficult part had been leaving Mississippi.

When he arrived in Chicago from Mississippi, he thought of staying there. Instead, at the urging of Mr. Washington, an old shoeshine man and confidant of Mildred, he decided to move to Akron. The fact that his friends from Mississippi would be there and Mr. Washington would be going made the move rather easy.

Mildred and Mr. Washington had arranged for Charlie's money to be transferred to a bank in Akron. All future checks would go through Chicago then on to the Akron bank. They had also arranged the purchase of a small building with two apartments upstairs and space for three businesses on the ground floor. It was decided that they would open a record shop in one and rent the other two spaces out. Charlie and Mr. Washington would each have an apartment upstairs.

"There it is, plain as day," said Johnathan. He pulled the car to the curb, parked, and pointed to a two-storey brick building directly across the street. Nestled between Razor's Edge

Barbershop on one side and East End Cleaners on the other was a record shop with a small sign that simply read, "Charlie's Records and Shoeshine".

"So that whole building belongs to Charlie?" asked Edward in absolute, utter amazement.

"Yup, the whole thing. The barbershop and the cleaners pay rent and Charlie and Mr. Washington live upstairs," answered Johnathan.

Jessie stepped from the car and stood staring at the building, more impressed than amazed.

"He didn't have enough sense to buy a decent place to live when he was in Mississippi" said Edward. "Now you telling me that he owns this whole building?" He stood there laughing at the irony of it all.

"I never knew he had that kind of money," said Johnathan with a touch of envy in his voice.

"Oh, Charlie's got a dollar or two," said Jessie.

They all hurried across the street to see their old friend.

"Not bad," said Jessie as he entered and glanced around at the well-stocked and tastefully decorated shop. Rows of records filled the back section of the shop. Large black and white photos of Billy Holiday, John Coltrane, and Miles Davis hung from the walls. Along the wall under the picture of John Coltrane was a row of three shoeshine chairs with foot stands.

"So this is what you did with all that money" said Edward. He was glad to see Charlie showing some signs of financial maturity.

Charlie had gained a little weight and added a bit of sophistication and confidence, but he was still the good friend they all remembered. As for Mr. Washington, Charlie introduced him as "the best little shoeshine man this side of heaven." He was an older gentleman with an angelic appearance. He was dressed in a white shirt, tie, and long apron. No one else seemed to notice, but to Edward there was something shocking about him. It wasn't his physical appearance but his presence. It was as if he were the presence, the being, or the spirit that Edward had felt since he arrived in Ohio. The sensation was almost overwhelming. *Who was this man? What was he,* wondered Edward?

"Come on. Let me show y'all the rest of the place," said Charlie proudly, appearing more and more like the businessman he had actually become.

"You all go ahead," said Mr. Washington as he grabbed Edward's shirtsleeve and held him in place. "Edward, you stay here and let me put a shine on those shoes for you. I think you need it."

Charlie quickly turned and looked at Mr. Washington, then at Edward. "Go ahead," said Charlie. "Let him knock some of that Mississippi mud off your shoes."

Charlie, Jessie, and Johnathan disappeared through a door leading to a flight of stairs. Edward took a seat in one of the chairs under the picture of Coltrane and placed his feet on the foot stand.

"My shoes look that bad?" joked Edward. He was puzzled by the offer and curious about the man. Mr. Washington ignored the question, walked over, and closed the door leading to the stairs. He lit two candles on the counter, then returned to stand in front of Edward. He stared down at his shoes.

"Well, how do they look?" asked Edward, now more confused than ever.

"Nice. Good leather. I see you believe in good shoes," answered Mr. Washington. He took a small brush, applied a little soap and water to it, and began gently scrubbing the dirt from Edward's shoes. "Here, push that foot forward a little," he said as he grabbed the back of Edward's shoe and pulled it towards him.

"Charlie sure was glad to see you and Jessie. He talks about you all the time. Y'all and Johnnie B." The little shoeshine man applied a little bleach to the brush and cleaned the stitching along the soles of Edward's shoes.

"I miss old Johnnie B.," said Edward. "He sure taught folks in Mississippi a thing or two."

"Johnnie B. was a good man," said Mr. Washington. "We all miss him, but God said it was Johnnie B.'s time."

"Yeah, but I don't believe Johnnie B. had to die like he did or when he did," said Edward.

"Regardless of what you believe, death is a necessary part of life," said Mr. Washington. "You don't have to believe in something for it to be true. It can be true even if you don't believe it."

He put down the brush, took a rag, and dried each shoe. He waited a few minutes for each shoe to completely dry, then applied a thin coat of black paste polish to each one. He stood back and watched as the polish was absorbed into the leather of the shoes and dried to a dull, cloudy finish.

"What about you, Edward, what do you believe?" he asked, looking directly at Edward for the first time instead of at his shoes.

Edward looked over at the picture of the smiling face of Billy Holiday on the opposite wall, then back at the soft-spoken little shoeshine man. Edward was one of the people who had a hard time dealing with death, especially the death of a friend or loved one.

"What do you believe?" repeated Mr. Washington, still looking directly at Edward.

"I believe life's too short and I believe Johnnie B. died too soon," answered Edward.

"Listen," said Mr. Washington. "Let me tell you a thing or two about life that Johnnie B. understood. He understood that life ain't too short, people just wait too long to start living it. He understood that when you live it, you should live it to its fullest. Johnnie B appreciated and embraced life. He knew that life can be short and that it can end suddenly. He also believed. He believed in the Good Book which says, 'He that believeth in the Son hath everlasting life; and he that believeth not the Son shall not see life; but the wrath of God abideth on him.' Johnnie B. believed that. What about you, Edward, what do you believe? Do you believe in the Good Book?"

Edward didn't answer. He just sat there staring down at Mr. Washington. Out of the corner of his eye, he could see the soft flicker of the candles on the counter, and he wondered who was this strange little man with the soul-searching questions? Who was he, really? What was he? Was he a preacher? Was he a prophet of some sort? Maybe even an angel. What? Whatever he was, thought Edward, he was definitely a man of God.

Mr. Washington leaned over and applied another thin coat of polish to Edward's shoes. "Yes, I am all that you think that I might be," he said, answering Edward's unspoken questions. He wiped his hands on his apron, then extended a hand to Edward. "Don't you know me? I was with Daniel in the lion's den. I was with Shadrach, Meshach, and Abednego when they were thrown into the fiery furnace. I am the one sent by the Lord to free Peter from jail and rescue him from Herod's clutches. I was one of the two who arrived at Sodom in the evening while Lot was sitting in the gateway of the city.

"When the high priest and all his associates arrested the apostles and put them in the public jail, I am the one who opened the doors of the jail and told them to go, stand in the temple courts, and tell the people the full message of this new life.

"I rolled back the rock and met Mary Magdalene at the tomb. It was I who told her that Jesus was not there, and he has risen. Don't you know me?" he asked.

Edward sat there, quiet and confused. Was this possible? Could the little shoeshine man actually be the angel he claimed to be? Edward didn't quite understand. More importantly, how could he believe in something that he didn't understand?

Mr. Washington sensed Edward's confusion and answered before he could finish forming the questions in his mind.

"Trust in the Lord with all your heart and lean not on your own understanding," said the little shoeshine man, quoting from the Bible. It is all quite possible. I am what you think I am and the one I profess to be."

Edward closed his eyes and leaned his head back against the wall, trying to make some sense out of all that was happening. Maybe this was true. He opened his eyes and looked down at the little shoeshine man staring up at him. Was this really an angel of the Lord?

"Yes, I am," said Mr. Washington, answering before Edward could ask.

There had never been any question about Edward's spirituality or his logic, but he could find no explanation for what was happening. Could Mr. Washington be the presence that he had felt since coming to Ohio?

"If you're truly God's angel, why are you here?" asked Edward. He was almost afraid to ask the question and equally afraid of what the answer might be.

Mr. Washington reached into the pouch of his apron and pulled out a small Bible. "The Good Book can answer all of your questions. All you have to do is know the Lord and believe." He turned to Luke chapter 4 verse 42 and started reading the answer to Edward's question. "'The people were looking for him and when they came to where he was He said, "I must preach the good news of the kingdom of God to the other towns also, because that is why I was sent."' Then from Romans 10:15, "'And how can they preach unless they are sent? As it is written, how beautiful are the feet of those who bring good news.' That's why I'm here, and that's why I shine shoes. And that's why I'm shining yours. Your news will be good news and benefit many."

He placed the Bible back into the pouch of his apron and looked up at Edward. "There's no reason to fear me or to fear my reasons for being here," he said. "We have always been with you, and surely He is with you always, to the very end of the age. Here, straighten out those feet," he said as he aligned Edward's shoes on the shoe stand. He put the scrub brush away and picked up a larger, softer polishing brush. He leaned forward and ran the brush back and forth along the sides of each shoe until the dull, cloudy finish slowly started to take on a soft glow like that of the candles. Mr. Washington smiled at the subtle transformation. He began to brush the shoes a little faster, back and forth along the backs and finally across the tops, faster and faster. He dipped his fingers into a small bowl of clean water and sprinkled a few drops onto the toe of each shoe. He continued to brush until the finish went from a soft glow to a nice shine.

"Does Charlie know who you are?" asked Edward as he watched the angel at work.

Mr. Washington put the brush aside and looked up at Edward. He smiled and slowly nodded his head as if wondering what had taken Edward so long to ask the question.

"Charlie knows me and he knows the Lord," answered Mr. Washington. "I hope you know the Lord. Knowing the Lord has saved Charlie, and that's the only way you can be saved. You see, your time on earth will end very soon. What matters is where you go next. Everyone will spend eternity somewhere. What about you, Edward? Where will you spend it?"

Edward didn't have an answer to the question, and Mr. Washington knew it. *They never do,* he thought. He reached into the shoebox and removed a small jar of his special polishing cream and a buffing cloth. With a piece of cotton from the pouch of his apron, he applied a thin coat of the polishing cream to the toe of each shoe. He buffed each shoe to a smooth, shiny, mirror-like finish. He stared down at Edward's shoes and smiled at his own reflection staring back at him.

"Well, how do they look?" he asked, pointing to the shiny, new-looking pair of shoes.

Edward glanced down at his shoes, impressed with the new look and the talent of the magical little shoeshine man.

"Look closer," said Mr. Washington. He wiped the buffing cloth across each shoe one more time.

Edward leaned forward and stared intently down at the mirror-like finish of his shoes. Instead of seeing his own reflection, Edward saw the smiling face of the little shoeshine man staring back at him. Suddenly, all that he thought was impossible became a reality. Edward sat straight up in his chair. He laid his head back against the wall and closed his eyes, unnerved and actually afraid of what he had just seen.

"Look closer," repeated Mr. Washington as he reached for the Bible in the pouch of his apron.

Despite his fear, Edward once again leaned forward and stared down at the reflection in his shoes. Nervous and with both hands holding tightly onto the arms of his chair, he leaned down further and looked closer. He had no idea what to expect. As he looked, the image in his shoes became clearer. As if from a distance, he could hear the pages of the Bible being turned as Mr. Washington searched for a passage to ease Edward's fear and explain what was happening.

The longer Edward stared at the reflection in his shoes, the less afraid he became. He relaxed his grip on the arms of the chair but still sat as if hypnotized by the image of little shoeshine man staring at him from his shoes.

"Can you hear me?" asked Mr. Washington.

Edward couldn't tell if the voice came from Mr. Washington or from the reflection in his shoes, but he heard it loud and clear. He turned and looked at the little shoeshine man, nodded, then stared back at the image in his shoes.

"Then listen," said Mr. Washington. Both he and the image in the shoes stared up at Edward. This time it was the image that spoke.

"You are special to God and he has blessed you and yours above all others. " said the image. You have spent your time on earth wisely, and you have obeyed God's commandments. Your time on earth will end soon, but it is only the beginning. God has forgiven you for your sins and you will be given new life. All that he asks of you is that you accept him as your Savior."

With that, the image in the shoes gradually faded away, and Edward was left staring down at Mr. Washington, who wiped the buffing cloth across each shoe one more time. After an agonizingly long few minutes, the image in the shoes re-appeared, and Edward knew that God was speaking to him through this little shoeshine man and the image in his shoes. He sat there quietly, ready to listen and do whatever was asked of him.

Mr. Washington smiled at Edward's realization, then once again aligned his shoes on the foot stand. "Are you ready to give your life to the Lord?" asked Mr. Washington.

Edward simply answered, "Yes."

"Do you accept Christ as your Savior?" asked the image.

Again Edward simply answered, "Yes."

The image continued to speak. "Lord, come upon us now and let your presence shine."

Mr. Washington opened his Bible to Psalms 80 and started reading at verse 19. "Restore us, Oh Lord God Almighty, Make you face shine upon us that we may be saved."

Slowly, the image in the shoes took on a slight glow and began to shine. Then, right there in that record shop, sitting in that shoeshine chair under the picture of Coltrane, Edward gave his life to the Lord and he was saved. There was no chorus of angels, no flashing, bright lights. It was just Edward, the image in the shoes, and Mr. Washington together in that record shop.

The image slowly began to fade, then it was gone. Edward was left shaken and short of breath. Mr. Washington, too, seemed shaken, but also excited about bringing another soul home to the Lord. They both remained silent as if waiting for the other to speak. Finally, Mr. Washington took a step up and sat down in the chair next to Edward. Edward took a deep breath and relaxed back into in his chair.

"I want to thank you," he said after his breathing returned to normal.

"For what?" asked Mr. Washington.

Edward couldn't answer right away. The entire experience had been just too emotional for him. He hesitated for a moment as a tear welled up in his eye and rolled down his cheek.

"For the shoeshine," he finally said, for lack of a better answer. He took another deep breath and wiped his hand across his forehead before continuing. "How much do I owe you?"

"Nothin', it was all paid for a long time ago," answered Mr. Washington. He stepped down from the chair and began putting the tools of his trade back into the shoeshine box. After each item had been carefully replaced, he tucked the box under his arm, then headed for the door leading upstairs. "Edward, you take care of yourself," said the little shoeshine man. "Regardless of what happens, everything's going to be all right."

Edward nodded in acknowledgement and started to stand as a show of respect.

"Don't get up" said Mr. Washington as he motioned for Edward to remain seated. "I'll send Charlie and them back down."

Just as Mr. Washington turned to leave, the door opened and Charlie, Jessie, and Johnathan entered from upstairs.

"Welcome back," said Mr. Washington. He walked over and held the door open for the three of them. Charlie walked past the counter to the row of chairs, stepped up, and sat in the chair next to Edward.

"Now that's what a pair of Florshiems should look like," he said and pointed to Edward's newly shined shoes. "Jessie, why don't you come up here and let Mr. Washington knock some of that Mississippi mud off your shoes?"

Jessie laughed, walked over, and looked at Edward's shoes. He stepped up and sat down in the remaining chair and looked at Mr. Washington in anticipation.

"Sorry gentlemen, not today," said Mr. Washington. I'm an old man and it's time I go upstairs and get some rest. Jessie, you come back tomorrow and I'll see what I can do for you." He removed his apron, loosened his tie, and bade good-bye to them all. He closed the door behind him, then started up the stairs. They all listened as the sound of his footsteps faded to silence.

So, through an angel and with an act as simple as a shoeshine, God had set in motion a series of events that would change their lives forever. He would test their faith, test their relationships, and test their friendship, all while demonstrating the awesome power of prayer.

CHAPTER X

Jesus wept.

John 11: 35

$\mathcal{I}$t was 8:00 in the evening on the twenty-seventh day of Mary Alice's arrival in Ohio and something was wrong. After nervously pacing back and forth in the tiny living room of her apartment, she finally sat down at the kitchen table. Edward had taken Doug to a baseball game in Cleveland, and they should have been back by now. Edward was a considerate man who would have called by now to explain any delay.

Something must be wrong. *Where in the world could they be?* she wondered. She buried her head in her hands and agonized over the short list of possibilities.

By 9:00 o'clock her nervousness had turned to fear. She stared up at the clock on the wall and watched as the seconds, then the minutes, slowly ticked away. Thirty minutes later, her fear turned to dread.

"Oh God," she said. "Where is Edward with my child?" She laid her head on the table and began to cry. Something was wrong and she could feel it. After a few minutes, she gathered herself and dried her eyes. She said a prayer, then stood up and looked around as if unsure of where she was.

"Get yourself together, girl," she said. She wiped her eyes one more time, then walked to the kids' room to check on David. At the entrance to the room she stopped and stared at Doug's empty bed. Immediately, that feeling of dread returned. She took a deep breath, walked into the room, and sat down on David's bed where he lay sleeping. Fighting back the tears, she leaned over and kissed him lightly on the forehead.

"Everything's going to be all right," she whispered, more to reassure herself than to comfort her sleeping child. She closed her eyes and prayed to God to bring the other half of her family home safely. At 10:00 p.m. she drifted off into an uneasy sleep.

Sophie and Johnathan were at home asleep, unaware of Mary Alice's situation. At 10:15 they were suddenly awakened by a series of loud knocks at their front door.

"Who is it?" shouted Johnathan.

Sophie sat up in the bed and rubbed her eyes as if trying to see the sound. "Who can that be at this time of night?" she asked, not really expecting an answer.

"Who is it?" Johnathan asked again, this time only louder. There was no answer, just a series of louder knocks. Then came his answer.

"It's the police," said an unfamiliar voice.

"The police? What in the world do they want?" asked Sophie. She and Johnathan both jumped from the bed, grabbed their robes, and went downstairs to answer the door. Johnathan hesitated at the door, then parted the curtains slightly. He peeked out and saw a uniformed police officer standing on the porch.

"It is the police," said Johnathan. He closed the curtain and looked at Sophie in disbelief.

"Well, open the door and see what they want," she said. Nervous almost to the point of trembling, Johnathan opened the door.

"Can I help you?" he asked.

"I'm officer Thomas," said the policeman. Are you Johnathan Perry?"

"Yes," answered Johnathan.

"Is there something wrong?" asked Sophie.

"Do you know Edward Graves?" asked the officer, ignoring Sophie's question.

"Yes, we know him," they both answered.

"What's happened?" asked Sophie.

"Are you family members of his?" asked the officer. "I need to know before I can give you any information," he explained.

Family members? thought Sophie. They were closer than family. She, Mary Alice, Lavern, and Minnie were friends in the truest, closest sense of the word. If one fell, the others were always there to pick her up. If something affected one, it affected them all. They had been like that since childhood, and had vowed to remain that way for a lifetime. It was a special kind of friendship that most people are never blessed enough to experience. If something was wrong, Sophie needed to know in order to help her friend.

"Yes, we're family," said Sophie. "He's my brother," she lied without the slightest bit of hesitation or guilt. "What's happened?" She grabbed Johnathan's arm and held on tightly as she waited for the answer.

"There's been an accident," said Officer Thomas.

Sophie felt her legs grow weak. She closed her eyes and leaned against Johnathan for support. "I have to sit down," she said. Johnathan led her to the sofa where they both sat down with Sophie still clutching his arm tightly.

"When did it happened?" she asked.

"It happened this evening just outside of Cleveland," said Officer Thomas. "A car crossed the center line of the highway and struck Mr. Graves's car head-on."

"Was there anybody with him?" asked Sophie. She closed her eyes, held her breath, and waited for the answer.

Officer Thomas paused. "May I sit down?" he asked. He appeared almost as distraught as Sophie. Before they could answer,

Officer Thomas took a seat in the nearest chair and continued. "It was just a terrible accident. The only survivor was a child in the car with Mr. Graves. They were the only two in his car. Mr. Graves died at the scene of the accident. The child is in critical condition, and they aren't sure if he's going to survive. I'm so very sorry ma'am. My heart goes out to your family."

Tears formed in the corners of Sophie's eyes, rolled down her cheeks, and met at her chin. There was silence, then a soft sobbing. Sophie was devastated beyond belief and she cried. She cried, not only because of what she had just heard, she cried because this might be more than Mary Alice could bear. God said that He would not put more on us than we could bear, but this might prove to be too much, she thought. So her tears flowed freely for her friend.

"How did you find us?" asked Johnathan.

"The address on Mr. Graves's driver's license was listed in Starkville, Mississippi. Inside his wallet was a piece of paper with your address and phone number written on it," explained Officer Thomas. "We didn't know if you were a relative or not, so that's why I came here instead of calling. Again, I'm terribly sorry for your loss. Is there anyone else you would like for me to notify?"

"No," said Sophie quickly. She released her grip on Johnathan's arm and tried to dry her eyes, but the tears continued to fall. "I'll make the calls."

"Are you sure?" asked Johnathan.

"I'm sure," said Sophie. She stood and started up the stairs. "I've got to call Minnie and Lavern. They'll tell Sam and Jessie. Then I've got to go to Mary Alice". Halfway up the stairs she stumbled, dropped to her knees, and stretched her arms above her head.

"Lord! Why, Lord? Why?" she screamed. She stood up, shaking her head, then continued up the stairs to call her friends.

Officer Thomas sat in silence as he watched Sophie and felt her pain. All that he had witnessed this evening would change his life forever. The image of the twisted wreckage, the critically injured child and Edward's lifeless body would be engraved in his mind forever. He could only imagine the effect this would have on the rest this family and their friends.

"I've got to go," said the officer as tears began to form in his eyes. He stood and shook Johnathan's hand. He reached into his pocket and removed a business card. On the back of the card he wrote a phone number, then gave it to Johnathan. "This is my home number. If there's anything I can do, anything, don't hesitate to call me."

He was truly sorry for their loss and it showed. He stood there, wanting to say more but not knowing what to say or how to say it. Finally he turned, said good-bye, and walked out of the door, knowing that somehow God would provide an answer to this tragedy.

Upstairs, Sophie fumbled through her dresser drawer until she found the phone numbers she was looking for. She held them tightly in her hand for a moment, then placed them on the table next to the phone. It was late but she knew the calls had to be made. She also knew that before she talked to anyone, she needed to talk to God. So, she lit a candle and turned off the lights. She got down on her knees and began to pray. There were going to be some difficult days ahead, but she was sure that God would hear her prayers and see them through this difficult time.

She prayed and she prayed. She prayed for God to send his angels. She prayed for Him to touch her friend and to shelter her from the storm that was about to engulf her life. She prayed for an angel to be a beacon of light, to shine in the darkness that had fallen over them in this midnight hour. She prayed that God would give each of them the strength and the faith of Job, so that like Job, they could come to know God's greatness. She prayed and she prayed and she prayed.

That night, God heard her prayers and the angels listened. In the heavens and on the earth, they listened. Reverend Johnson in Starkville listened. The old man on the farm in Starkville listened. Mr. Washington paced the floor in his apartment above the record shop and he listened. Lavern's daughter, Julie, lay asleep in her bed and she listened. Francis, the nurse at the hospital watching over Doug, listened. All the angels listened and they understood how great her suffering was.

Finally her prayers stopped, but the next morning they would continue. They would continue until God eventually answered them. Sophie laid her head down against the edge of the bed. She started to cry but quickly dried her tears. She knew that now was the time for the strength she had prayed for.

At 11:15 p.m. she got up and walked over to the table to make her phone calls. With trembling hands, she picked up the telephone and called Minnie. Due to the lateness of the call and the strain in Sophie's voice, Minnie knew immediately that something was wrong. Sophie did not try to disguise the pain she felt; she merely gave Minnie the news exactly as she had received it from Officer Thomas. Minnie reacted calmly, much as Sophie had expected, but the pain and the agony were obvious. Minnie's only question was which child was it, Doug or David?

Sophie suddenly realized that she didn't know. Minnie understood.

"You just take care of Mary Alice until I get there," said Minnie. "I'll be leaving as soon as I pack." Sophie heard her call Sam's name just before the phone disconnected.

Sophie dropped her head and thanked God for her friend. She decided to take a little time to collect her thoughts before making her next call. She knew that her call to Lavern would be more difficult than her call to Minnie had been. Lavern's reaction would be more emotional and not as calm. At 11:45 she picked up the phone and called Lavern. Like Minnie, Lavern knew immediately that something was wrong.

"Dear God, what's wrong?" she asked, her voice already filled with emotion.

"There's been an accident," answered Sophie. "It's Edward and one of the kids. I don't know if it's Doug or David. It's bad, Lavern, real bad. I already called Minnie."

"Oh Lord," shouted Lavern. "Where's Mary Alice?"

"She's at home," answered Sophie. "She doesn't know yet."

Sophie told her about the police officer. She explained how he had found her name and address on a piece of paper in Edward's wallet. She then proceeded to give Lavern an account of what happened. She gave it exactly as Officer Thomas had given it to her and just as she had given it to Minnie.

"This can't be happening," said Lavern. "It's not possible." Then Lavern started crying. The tears started and she was unable to stop them. Sophie closed her eyes and once again prayed for God to grant them the strength to see them through this difficult time.

Finally, Lavern gained control of herself. "What are we going to do?" she asked. "How are we going to tell Mary Alice? What do we say? When do we tell her? Shouldn't we get her to the hospital? You know she don't drive. Can't we call the hospital and see which child is there?" The questions, like her tears, flowed continuously. "Oh God, what are we going to do?"

Then there was silence except for the occasional sound of Lavern crying.

"Listen," said Sophie. "I'm going to the hospital and find out if it's Doug or David. I'll call you from there and tell you who it is and how he's doing."

"What about Mary Alice?" asked Lavern. "We can't tell her something like this over the telephone." Like Sophie, Lavern worried that this might be more that Mary Alice could bear, so she wanted to be there with her friend to help in any way she could.

"You put on some coffee and I'll come over when I leave the hospital. We can go talk to her together," said Sophie.

"Okay," agreed Lavern. "Jessie should be home from work by then. I'll tell him and he can watch the kids while we go. This is going to be real hard on him too. You know how close him and Edward were."

"I know," said Sophie. She hung the phone up and sat there, trembling, debating whether to go to Mary Alice's now or after she left the hospital.

When Sophie went downstairs, Johnathan had fallen asleep on the couch. Sophie looked in on her son, then decided to let him and his father sleep. At midnight, Sophie grabbed her Bible, her purse, and car keys and left for the hospital. The streets were deserted and Sophie felt alone. Not just alone in her car, or alone in the streets, but alone in the world. It was a world that now seemed empty, void of everything but sorrow. It was a world she hardly recognized. It was a world that had suddenly turned against her friend with a fury that was almost incomprehensible. Where was God at a time like this, she wondered. She clutched her Bible in one hand while driving with the other. Once again she started to cry. She held her Bible to her chest and prayed, trusting that God would answer her prayers and give comfort to her friend.

Sophie stopped her car at a traffic light. She was the only car on the street. *Why am I stopping,* she wondered. Off in the distance she could see the hospital, and her thoughts turned to the child inside fighting for his life.

"Lord," she prayed. "A life has been taken from us and another one hangs delicately by your hand. Be merciful, O Lord. Be merciful. Give us the strength to accept your will and let your will be done."

At 12:15 a.m., Mary Alice woke up and walked into the living room. She looked out the window, hoping to see Edward's car pulling up into the parking lot. She started to call Lavern but decided against it. It was late and Edward would probably be here in a few minutes, she thought. She tried her best to convince herself that everything was fine, but she knew it wasn't. She walked back to the children's room and resumed her restless sleep.

At 12:30 a.m., Sophie arrived at the hospital. Once inside, she walked directly towards the nurses' station. The nurse on duty saw her approaching and immediately stood up to greet her.

"Are you here about the Graves child, Douglas Lee Graves?" she asked.

That answered Sophie's first question. It was Doug and not David. "Yes I am," she said. "How did you know his name?"

"He regained consciousness long enough to tell us his name. He said his mother's name was Mary Alice. Is that you?"asked the nurse.

"No. My name's Sophie and I'm a friend," she said. "How's he doing?"

"They just took him to surgery again," answered the nurse. "His condition is still critical. The doctors are doing everything they can to save him, but now it's all in the hands of the Lord. The only thing we can do is pray and wait. He's a tough little kid and he's holding on."

Sophie felt her knees weaken and staggered over to the closest chair. The nurse took her by the arm and helped her sit down. Sophie sat there, somewhat numb, all thoughts on Doug. Finally her emotions took control. She was unable to hold back the tears that welled up in her eyes and she cried uncontrollably.

"It's okay. Everything's going to be all right," said the nurse. She sat down on the arm of the chair and gently patted Sophie on the back, then looked around as if for assistance. "You sit here. I'll be right back."

A few minutes later, the nurse returned with a glass of water and a cold, damp hand towel. Sophie took a sip of the water and the nurse placed the towel across the back of her neck. Sophie folded her arms across her lap and laid her head down.

"I'm sorry," she said. "I just don't know what to do. This has been just terrible."

"Where's his mother? Does she know about this?" asked the nurse.

"No," replied Sophie.

The nurse was shocked by the answer. "Listen to me," she said. "If you're Mary Alice's friend, you need to go tell her what's happened. You need to get her here as soon as you can. If there's any other friends, call them and bring them too. She's going to need all the support and prayers she can get."

"I am her friend," replied Sophie.

The nurse could tell that they were friends, best friends. She also sensed that because of that friendship, Sophie was unknowingly trying to protect her friend from the reality of all that had happened. "Then please, please listen to me and do as I say. It's very important," she said. "There isn't much time. I'll be here watching over the child while you go get his mother."

Sophie slowly raised her head from her lap and looked up at the nurse. She wondered who was this person who had suddenly made things so clear and seemed to know so much. She took the towel from her neck, dried her eyes, and wiped her face with it. She would do as she was told.

"Thank you for everything," she said as she handed the towel to the nurse. "Is there a phone I can use?"

"Yes there is," answered the nurse. Come with me."

Sophie followed the nurse down the hall to a small office.

"You can use the phone in here," said the nurse. As she was leaving, she turned and gave Sophie one final instruction. "Before you call, open your Bible to the book of John and read chapter 14, verses 13 and 14." Then she was gone.

Sophie closed the door and sat down. She opened her Bible and started reading the indicated verses.

"And I will do whatever you ask in my name, so that the Father may be glorified in the name of the Son. You may ask me for anything in my name, and I will do it."

Sophie sat there meditating on the importance of what she had just read. Her faith was strong and she believed with all her heart that God would do as he said. She closed he eyes, bowed her head, and made her request. She asked God to send an angel to watch over Doug, to keep him safe until Mary Alice arrived. Little did she know, her prayer had already been answered.

At 1:00 a.m., Sophie closed her Bible and called Lavern. Lavern answered on the first ring.

"Sophie, is that you?" she asked.

"It's me," said Sophie. "Doug's the one. I'll be there in a few minutes. We need to go to Mary Alice."

CHAPTER XI

The righteous cry out, and the Lord hears them; he delivers them from all their troubles. The Lord is close to the brokenhearted and saves those who are crushed in spirit.

Psalm 34:17,18

At 2:00 a.m., Mary Alice was awakened by a knock at her door. Sophie and Lavern stood outside, stoically waiting for their friend to answer. Unlike the loud knocking that had awakened Sophie and Johnathan, this was a soft tapping sound. The messenger was different but the message would be the same. Mary Alice immediately sat up in bed, wondering who could it be. She knew it couldn't be Edward because he wouldn't be knocking. Regardless, she jumped up from the bed and ran to answer the door, hoping against all hope that it was Edward and Doug. She flung the door open and stood staring at the expressionless faces of her two friends. They walked in and closed the door behind them without saying a word. Something was terribly wrong, and Mary Alice knew it. She reached out, grabbed Sophie's hand, and held onto it tightly.

"What's happened?" She asked. "What is it?"

Sophie and Lavern glanced at each other then looked at Mary Alice.

"It's Edward, isn't it?" asked Mary Alice.

"Yes," said Sophie. "Come on, sit down."

The three of them sat down on the couch with Mary Alice still holding on tightly to Sophie's hand.

"We need to get you to the hospital," said Sophie. Her voice was soft, almost a whisper. By the tone of her friend's voice, Mary Alice knew she should prepare herself for the worst.

"How bad is it?" she asked, her voice quivering and barely audible. As hard as she tried, she was not prepared for her friend's answer.

"It' bad, real bad," said Sophie. "Edward and Doug were in a car wreck outside of Cleveland late this evening. Doug is in the hospital and we've got to get you there as soon as we can."

"What about Edward?" asked Mary Alice. "What about Edward?"

Sophie hesitated before answering. That hesitation was enough to let Mary Alice know what her friends didn't want to tell her.

"I'm sorry," said Sophie. "Edward died in the accident."

Lavern bowed her head and started to cry again. Mary Alice opened her mouth to scream at God and condemn Him for taking her husband, but there was no sound. Her eyes opened wide and rolled back in her head, and she fainted. There are some things that God does not permit. She fell back on the couch, still clutching Sophie's hand. She lay there, her chest heaving as she fought to breathe. Seeing her friend faint, Lavern screamed the question but not the condemnation that Mary Alice was unable to speak..

"God, why, why, why?!" She screamed the word over and over.

Lavern's screams woke David. His first thought was of the monster. Had it left Mississippi and somehow found its way to Ohio? Had it crashed through their door and was now in the apartment? Who had screamed and why? He had no idea of what had happened or of the real tragedy that had visited his family. He started to cry. He climbed down from his bed and ran to the living room, a scared and confused six-year-old boy expecting a monster to appear at any moment.

Lavern began fanning Mary Alice with a newspaper taken from the coffee table. She and Sophie sat there with their friend as she slowly regained consciousness. Finally Mary Alice opened her eyes, sat up, and saw David standing there.

"Come here, baby," she said as she reached out for him, her hands shaking. She realized that not only had she lost a husband, and possibly a son, but David had lost his father and maybe his only brother. David ran to his mother and threw himself into her arms, finally feeling safe amid all the confusion.

"It's okay," she whispered. "It's okay. She held him tightly, then kissed him on the top of his head.

"We've got to go," she said. Still holding onto David, Mary Alice failed in her first attempt to stand. She fell back onto the couch and started to cry. It was almost more than she could bear.

"Let me take David," said Lavern. "I'll be right back."

Lavern took David to her apartment, then she and Sophie helped Mary Alice to the car. They rode through the empty streets to the hospital without speaking. The only sound was the crying and praying of Mary Alice as she called on the Lord. She was like Job in chapter 3 verse 25: "What I feared has come upon me; what I dread has happened to me. I have no peace, no quietness; I have no rest, only turmoil."

Sophie stopped at the same traffic light as before and stared at the hospital off in the distance. She gripped the steering wheel tightly with both hands and she prayed. She prayed that God had sent his angel to watch over Doug while she was gone. She prayed that peace would come to her friend. Suddenly, she couldn't wait for the light to change and she drove through it. For some reason it seemed more important than ever that they get to the hospital as soon as possible.

At the same, time Jessie was at home on the phone talking to Charlie. He told him about the accident and the death of their friend. Charlie called Mr. Curry, the grocery store owner, and told him. His wife, Sarah, went next door and woke Flora, the school crossing guard, and told her. Flora called her brother, who told his wife. He then called Mitch the mailman and told him of the accident. Soon phones were ringing and lights were coming on all over the projects. Word of the death of a good man spreads quickly, and Edward was a good man.

After making his last call, Jessie grabbed a beer from the icebox and walked outside to the parking lot. He sat on the hood of his car, took a long sip from his beer, then stared up at the sky. He searched the sky, as if searching for God to confront him on his decision to take such a good man. Finally, he finished his beer and walked back inside. He knelt down next to his bed and said a prayer for Mary Alice and her family. Then, for the first time in many, many years, he cried. He cried because a good man had died, and he cried because he had lost a true friend.

At three o'clock that morning, Sophie arrived back at the hospital with her friends. Mary Alice had stopped crying and dried her eyes. She knew that for the sake of her kids and for her own sanity, she had to be strong. She had to have faith and believe that God would see her through this terrible time. She knew God was a good God. He had taken her husband, but she was sure he would not take her son. She prayed for God's mercy and his grace. Her faith, unlike her spirit, was shaken but not broken. Even with her renewed inner strength, Sophie and Lavern still had to help her from the car and up the steps to the hospital entrance. Once inside, they were met by the nurse who had promised to watch over Doug.

"He's out of surgery. He's back in his room and resting," said the nurse. She seemed relieved but still concerned. "You must be Mary Alice, the child's mother." She extended her hand.

"Yes," answered Mary Alice. She took the nurse's hand in hers and held it tightly.

"I'm Francis," said the nurse. "If there's anything I can do, just let me know."

"Can I see my child?" asked Mary Alice.

"Yes, but he's still in very critical condition," said Francis. "He won't be able to hear you and he can't speak. Like I told your friend, he's a tough little kid and he's holding on, but it's all in God's hands now."

"That's all I can ask for," said Mary Alice. "Where is he?"

"He's upstairs in ICU," answered Francis. "Come with me and I'll take you up there."

Francis led them upstairs to Doug's room. He lay there in bed attached to a monitor with a breathing tube in his mouth, intravenous tubes in his arms, and his head wrapped in gauze. His breathing was labored and his face was swollen almost beyond recognition. Even with the support of her friends, Mary Alice fell to her knees at the sight of her child.

"My baby, my baby," she whispered. The tears once again streamed down her face as she teetered on the verge of collapse.

"Come on over here and sit down," said Sophie as she tried to pull Mary Alice to her feet. Mary Alice gathered what little strength she had left and stood. She leaned over and kissed Doug on his bandaged forehead, then turned and sat in the chair next to his bed. She closed her eyes and sat there, slowly rocking back and forth, calling on the Lord.

Lavern sat in the chair next to Mary Alice while Sophie stood and stared down at Doug in disbelief. Like Mary Alice, she knew God was a good God, but why in God's name had he let this happen? She prayed that God would be merciful and not take this child.

Minutes later, Francis returned with two more chairs. She gave one to Sophie and sat in the other. Lost in their own thoughts, each of them sat silently, their eyes fixed on Doug. All too soon, Francis started to feel the life slowly slipping away from Doug. She knew something had to be done. She slid her chair closer to the three of them and they all held hands. Everyone bowed her head and Francis began to pray. All through the early morning hours she prayed. She prayed for God to "touch this child and give him just a little more time. Don't take him yet." She prayed for God to give Mary Alice rest, that she might be strong in her body and in her spirit.

Once again, God heard and the angels listened as prayers were offered up for Mary Alice and her child. However, this time they listened as one of their own called upon the Lord. As a result, just before dawn, God assembled his angels before him and the Angel of the Lord was among them. They all were given instructions and specific assignments to carry out. Then the angels went out from the presence of the Lord. By sunrise Doug was breathing a little easier and his condition seemed to have stabilized.

Finally Francis stood, walked over, and removed the chart from Doug's bed. She read it and compared it to the monitor, then she silently thanked God for answering her prayers. She started to explain the change in Doug's condition to Mary Alice, but decided against it.

"Can I get you anything?" she asked instead.

"Yes, please. We'll have some black coffee," said Sophie, answering for the three of them. She followed Francis out into the hallway and stood there silently while Francis updated Doug's chart.

"Is there anything we need to know?" Sophie asked once Francis was finished with the chart.

"Yes, know that our prayers are being heard. Tell Mary Alice not to worry," she said. "God will take care of it all in his own way." She looked at Sophie and saw the compassion and concern that she felt for her friend. Francis wanted to explain everything to her, to make it all clear. She wanted to tell her that God had already made his decision. She wanted to tell her God's plans for Mary Alice. But as much as she wanted to, she knew that she couldn't. God would do that in his own time and in his own way.

They had all witnessed one of life's ultimate tragedies—the tragedy of a woman, suddenly and without warning, losing her husband. Then before she could recover from that terrible loss, they watched as that same woman prayed for God not to take her child. Francis stood silently for a few long moments. She gave Sophie a hug , then left to get the coffee.

Feeling somewhat reassured, Sophie went back into the room. Mary Alice sat in her chair with her head laid back and her eyes closed. Sophie couldn't tell if she had fainted again or was asleep. Either way, she would get some rest. Lavern stood leaning against the windowsill, staring out the window.

"Doug seems to be doing a little better," said Lavern without turning around. "It's almost as if God heard that nurse's prayers."

"I hope He did," said Sophie. "What about you? How you doin'?"

"I'm okay," answered Lavern. She turned and stared down at Doug. She closed her eyes then shook her head. "No, I'm not," she confessed. "I'm worried about Mary Alice. She already lost her husband, and if that child dies, I'm afraid she might lose her mind. She loved that man and them kids more than life itself."

"I know," said Sophie. She walked over and stood next to Lavern. She looked down at her wrist and noticed for the first time that she had forgotten her watch. She looked up at the sun to try to get some idea of the time, but she couldn't tell. For some reason, the sun didn't look the same as it did in Mississippi.

"What time is it?" she asked.

"It's about 7:30 in the morning," answered Lavern.

Sophie stood there, staring up at the sun. It had been a long and difficult night for them all, and it was starting to take its toll.

"I can't believe I've been up all night," said Sophie. "I haven't been up this long since my last night in Mississippi. Me and Minnie sat up all night talking and watched the sun come up." She paused and thought back to that morning. "That was the last time I saw Minnie. I miss our friend," she said wistfully.

Minutes later Francis returned with Doug's chart still in her hands and no coffee.

"Why don't you two let Mary Alice and Douglas get some rest and come down to the lobby with me?" she said. "There's something I want you to see."

Sophie and Lavern both looked at Mary Alice, still sitting with her head laid back and eyes closed.

"You two go ahead," said Lavern. "I'll stay here with Mary Alice. I don't want her to wake up and find nobody here with her."

"She'll be all right," said Francis. "Trust me."

They looked at each other, then back at Mary Alice. Reluctantly, they left her and followed Francis down the stairs to the lobby. All the way down to the lobby, it seemed they could hear voices. Once they reached the lobby, they were greeted by a crowd of about 25-30 people.

"What is this?" whispered Sophie. "All these people."

There was Charlie with Mr. Washington, Mr. Curry the grocery store owner and his wife. There was Mitch the mailman and Jessie with the kids. There was Officer Thomas, the policeman who first told them about the accident. There were some they only knew in passing and others they had never seen before. Regardless, they had all gathered there for the same reason. They were there out of concern for Mary Alice and Doug.

Sarah the grocery store owner's wife stepped forward. She glanced around as if waiting for someone to join her.

"Charlie called and told me and Roger about the accident," she said. "After that, word just sort of spread. If there's anything we can do, just let us know."

"That's right," murmured the crowd in agreement.

"Anything at all!" shouted a voice from the rear.

Francis looked out over the crowd and knew that God was at work. She smiled as she recognized Julie and Mr. Washington. Julie stood there holding little David's hand, watching over him, just as God had instructed her to do. There were other angels out there and she was glad. They all had their own instructions and assignments from God to carry out. Francis closed her eyes and thanked God for sending his angels in this time of need. Sometimes even an angel needs help and now was one of those times.

Jessie walked up to Lavern with the kids. He gave her a long hug and a quick kiss on the cheek.

"How's the boy doing?" he asked.

"He's doing a little better but it doesn't look good," answered Lavern.

"What about Mary Alice?" he asked.

"That's another story," said Lavern. "She's upstairs asleep right now. She knows God will get her through this."

"I hope God helps us all get through this," said Jessie. Lavern could see the devastation in her husband at the loss of his friend. He and Edward were like brothers and they had been that way since childhood. She wanted to speak but couldn't find the words. Instead, she knelt down and extended her arms to David. "Come here, baby," she said.

David's reaction was to move closer to Julie.

"He's been that way since we left the apartment," said Jessie. "Julie talked to him while I was outside. When I came back, he was holding onto her hand and he hasn't let go since."

"Does he know what's happened?" she asked.

"He knows," said Jessie. "Julie told him."

Francis walked over and placed her hand on David's shoulder, then looked down into his eyes.

"Do you know me?" she asked.

"Yes," he answered. "Julie told me about you."

"Everything's going to be all right," said Francis.

"I know," said David.

Francis kissed him on top of the head, then stood and once again looked out over the crowd.

"Listen everybody," she said. "Mary Alice and Doug are both resting. Doug is out of surgery and doing better. He hasn't regained consciousness yet but his vital signs have improved. Now, it's all in the hands of the Lord. I want you all to go home and let them rest. When you get home, I want you to light a candle and say a prayer for both of them. I want you to tell you friends, your neighbors, and your family to pray. Please, please, it is important that you do this. If you do, I promise you, God will answer."

The crowd grew quiet. There was no sound, no movement or immediate response. They were as statues, unblinking, looking up at Francis. Finally there was a voice from the crowd.

"Will God hear us?" asked the voice. "Will he truly hear us?"

"He will hear you," said Francis. "There is power in the prayers of the righteous and God hears their cries."

"Then we'll do it," said another voice, a little louder and with conviction.

Slowly the crowd began to disperse until the only ones left were Jessie and the kids. David stood there, still holding Julie's hand while little Alfred stood close by.

"It's been a long night for everybody," said Francis. Why don't you all go home and get some rest."

"Sophie, you go home," said Lavern. "Jessie, you take the kids with you and look after them. I'll stay here. I can't leave Mary Alice here by herself. I just can't do it. She's been through too much." Lavern's voice began to quiver and a tear rolled down her cheek. It was all she could do to keep from crying out loud . She composed herself then turned to Francis. "Can you put a cot or something in Doug's room for Mary Alice? She's the one who needs the rest. She ain't goin' to leave her child and I ain't goin' to leave her."

Francis understood. There were cots and rollaway beds expressly for situations like this.

"I'll have one brought up," she said. "What about you? Is there anything I can get you?"

"Just a cup of black coffee and one for Mary Alice," answered Lavern.

Francis smiled, turned, and started toward the cafeteria. Walking down the hall, all she could think about was the child upstairs clinging to life and the mother who would not leave his side. "I'll meet you upstairs," she said without looking back.

Sophie walked over and hugged Lavern. "Take care of you," she said. "I'll be back later. Minnie and Sam should be here tonight. You try to get some rest and call me if there's any change or if you need anything."

Jessie shook his head, gathered the kids, and started for the door. The tears had started to fall once again, and he didn't want the women to see him cry. Life was not meant to be this way, he thought. How could God let something like this happen? He just didn't understand God. More importantly, how could he believe in something that he didn't understand?

Lavern watched as Jessie held the kids close and walked out the door. Sophie turned and followed them out, leaving Lavern alone in the lobby. She stood there, her head bowed, fighting to hold back the tears. Finally, she took a deep breath and went upstairs to see about her friend.

Chapter XII

Jesus said, "Let the little children come to me, and do not hinder them, for the kingdom of heaven belongs to such as these.

Matthew 19: 14

Sophie returned to the hospital early that afternoon. Once there, she literally had to force Lavern to go home and get some rest. Lavern reluctantly agreed, but only after vowing to return in a few hours. It was like that; one would leave and the other would return. That continued until Minnie arrived from Mississippi late that night. From then on, the three of them vowed to remain with Mary Alice until God either took Doug or gave him back. Occasionally Francis would join them. They would all form a circle and hold hands and Francis would lead them in prayer.

In the projects, signs that read, "Pray for Mary Alice and Doug" began appearing in windows. Mitch the mailman passed out cards with the same message. The message quickly spread through the projects. Everyone prayed and they prayed and they prayed. The children even began to sing their own little song of prayer.

God our Father, in heaven above,
This prayer is from your children, the children you love.

Douglas Lee Graves is like our brother,
So we pray for him and we pray for his mother.

All the while, God heard and the angels listened.

By the morning of the third day, there seemed to be a slight improvement in Doug's condition. Mary Alice noticed but was cautiously optimistic. However, her optimism did little to alleviate the pain caused by the loss of her husband. It was a loss from which she would never fully recover.

Since the accident, Mary Alice had gotten very little rest. Sleep would come, but she would cry herself awake. Her waking hours were filled with thoughts of her husband and the agonizing fear of losing her child. Pain now seemed to be the only constant in her life. Had it not been for the prayers and support of her friends, she might have let go.

At 11:30 that morning, Jessie arrived at the hospital with the kids for the first of his twice-a-day visits. Sophie, Minnie, and Lavern met him in the lobby.

"Where's Mary Alice?" he asked. "It's kind of strange seeing the three of you without her."

"She's upstairs," answered Lavern. "Francis sent us down here. She wanted to talk to Mary Alice alone."

Jessie looked at the three of them, then at David still holding Julie's hand. "Come on," he said. "Let's get a cup of coffee and a snack for the kids."

Upstairs, Mary Alice watched as Francis took the readings from the monitor and updated Doug's chart. Francis seemed somewhat nervous and Mary Alice asked her what was wrong.

Francis placed her fingers across her lips. "Just be still," was all she said. She walked over, closed the door, and locked it. She returned to her chair and sat down without explaining. Mary Alice looked at her, wondering what in the world was going on.

Just then, Doug made a barely audible coughing sound. Mary Alice looked at Doug then back at Francis, who simply bowed her head and closed her eyes. Doug coughed again and raised his head slightly. Mary Alice rushed to his side and whispered, "Doug, can you hear me, baby?" He opened his eyes and tried to speak, but there was no sound. Mary Alice leaned closer and whispered his name again, then asked the same question. "Can you hear me, baby?"

He looked at her, but was still unable to speak. His head fell back onto the pillow and he lay there, motionless. The room grew eerily quiet. The only sound was Doug's labored breathing. Finally, Doug took a deep breath, his eyes closed, and with a long sigh, he exhaled his last earthly breath.

At 11:52 that morning, Douglas Lee Graves, the oldest child of Mary Alice and the late Edward Lee Graves, died.

Mary Alice couldn't take life anymore and she simply let go. "Oh God! Not my child!" she cried out. "Please God, please, don't take my baby! No, no, no!" She raised her hands above her head and fell to the floor, unconscious. It was too much for her to take.

Just as she lost her hold on life and was about to slip away, God reached out and grabbed her. He wrapped her in his arms and held her close so she couldn't let go. He held her, just as he held Mitch the mailman when his wife died during the birth of their second child. He held her, just as he held Flora, the school crossing guard, when her only sister died from a stroke. He held her, just as he holds us all during those difficult times in our lives.

Francis watched, then fell to her knees beside Mary Alice. She extended her arms and tilted her head back. With her eyes filled with tears, she stared upwards towards the heavens, silently crying out to the Lord. All across the heavens and across the earth, angels looked to the Lord. One of their own was crying and they all felt her pain.

Downstairs, tears filled little Julie's eyes. She gently squeezed David's hand and whispered what was happening in his ear. In the apartment above the record shop, Mr. Washington wiped the tears from his eyes and dropped to his knees. Reverend Johnson in Starkville opened his Bible and read the 23rd Psalm as his tears dampened the pages. The old man in Starkville knelt at the bench by the pond and cried.

There is a cry that only God can hear. It is the cry of his angels. That morning, when Doug died, God heard that cry. It was like the soft cry of a newborn baby in the middle of the night that wakes a mother from her sleep. It was like the bleating of a lamb, hiding in fear, softly calling for its mother. Like those mothers, God alone hears the cries of his children. God knew, as He always does, what had to be done. He once again assembled his angels before him, and the Angel of the Lord was once again among them. The angels were instructed to go to earth, deliver a word, and let God's presence be known. Then the angels went out from the presence of the Lord.

Mary Alice lay there on that cold hospital floor clinging to the Lord. All that she believed in was gone. How could a gracious God be so cruel? What had she done to deserve this? Had she angered God in some way? Life was deserting her, and now she could only speak through her spirit.

"Precious Lord, precious Lord, please help me," was all her spirit could say.

Suddenly, the room was filled with a bright light, then there was darkness and God's presence filled the room. Mary Alice felt the presence and her spirit found comfort in it. Her eyes opened slightly, but she was unable to see. Then a voice from the darkness spoke to her spirit.

"Close your eyes and you will see me," said the voice.

Her eyes closed and she saw an angel standing before her, and she was afraid. The angel spoke to Mary Alice as Gabriel had spoken to Mary of Nazareth.

"Greetings, you who are highly favored! Do not be afraid, Mary Alice, for you have found favor with God. I am the Angel of the Lord. I stand in the presence of the Lord. Angels have cried for you and your child. God has heard their cries. You have asked questions of God and I have been sent to give you answers.

"But why?" asked Mary Alice. "Why didn't God hear my cries and answer my prayers?"

"You have been faithful to God and kept his commandments. For this your prayers have been answered," said the Angel of the Lord. "God says in Jeremiah 29:12, 'Then you will call and come and pray to me, and I will listen to you. You will seek me and find me. When you seek me with all your heart, I will be found by you.' Our God is a good and gracious God. He hears the cries of the righteous and he answers their prayers."

Once again Mary Alice spoke through her spirit. "It is true, I have been faithful to God and kept his commandments. He has blessed my life, but now those blessings have been taken from me. My life is now filled with sorrow and grief. My soul aches and my heart is broken. My life is slipping away, and now I can speak only through my spirit. Will God ever ease this pain? He has taken my husband and my child. He has taken more than I can bear to give. How can God be so greedy?"

The Angel of the Lord answered, "You have heard of Job's perseverance and seen what the Lord finally brought about. Did not Job lose seven sons and three daughters? Did he not lose seven thousand sheep, three thousand camels, five hundred yoke of oxen, and five hundred donkeys? Was he not the greatest man of the East? Did he not maintain his faith after losing everything? His faith was fearless. In all this, Job sinned not nor charged God foolishly. Like Job, you have lost much, but God has given more. God gave his all to forgive your sins that you might come to believe. For God so loved the world that he gave his only begotten Son, and whosoever believeth in him shall not perish but have everlasting life."

Mary Alice listened to the Angel through her spirit, then her spirit spoke. "Like Job, I feel it would have been better had I not been born than to endure a lifetime of the pain I now feel. Today the pain is worse than it was yesterday and less than it will be tomorrow. Have I not suffered enough? The joy I once knew is no more. A darkness has replaced the light, and now I close my eyes to see. My life, along with my husband's and my child's, has ended."

"Your child and your husband are special to God and there is much for them to do," said the Angel of the Lord. "They have not perished but will have everlasting life. This is not their ending nor yours, but a new beginning. It is all part of God's plan. You will be blessed above all others"

Once again, Mary Alice spoke through her spirit. "I have but one son left and I am afraid for him. Have I angered God in some way? Will he take my last child and make my loss complete?

"Like you, David is highly favored by the Lord," answered the Angel of the Lord. "He will live long and prosper. Years from now people will speak of your suffering and how your faith endured. They will speak of David and of his greatness. He will grow to be a leader among men, and his greatness will be known throughout the land. This is the word from the Lord."

Then there was silence. Gradually the darkness gave away to the light, and the Angel of the Lord was gone.

When the angel was gone back into heaven, Mary Alice was awakened by the Spirit. Francis reached out and helped her to her feet. Mary Alice rubbed her eyes and stared at the lifeless body of her son.

"My baby, my baby" she whispered. Tears fell, but the presence of the Lord still filled the room and she was comforted by it. Francis led Mary Alice to a chair, then sat down next to her.

"I saw an angel," said Mary Alice. "Did you see him?"

"Yes, he was here," answered Francis. She walked over and unlocked the door, opened it, then returned to her seat. "The angels serve God's purpose. In all God does there is purpose. He has a purpose for you, and in time you will come to know it. For now, trust in the Lord, believe in angels, and know that there are people who love you very much. God has placed those people in your life for a reason."

"Is there a reason for God to take people from our lives?" asked Mary Alice. She thought of Edward and Doug.

"Yes," answered Francis. "But only God knows the reason. Each of you must eventually leave this earth, and when you leave, each of you is taken from someone's life. Therefore, do as much good as you can in the time God provides you. Help someone, be a friend to someone, touch someone, pray for someone, teach someone, be a positive example for someone, love your family, cherish your time with them, love God with all your heart, but most of all, live life according to God's commandments. If you do these things, God's grace will fill your life. Then, you will not only be blessed, but you will be a blessing to others."

Francis stood and walked over to Doug's bed. She removed the tubes and detached the monitor. *God knows,* thought Francis, *no one should ever have to experience the death of their child.*

Mary Alice joined Francis at Doug's bed. She kissed him lightly on the forehead, then slowly pulled the sheet over his head and said a prayer. When they finished, Mary Alice turned and hugged Francis.

"Thank you for everything," she said. Mary Alice was still consumed with the Spirit and had not fully returned to herself.

"You're welcome," said Francis. "Come on, let's get you home so you can get some rest. I'll take care of everything here."

"When I was little, my mother told me there's an angel that watches over me," said Mary Alice as they headed for the lobby. "She told me that if I'm ever in need, if I ever lose my way and feel that life has gotten the best of me, I should call my angel. She never told me the angel's name."

"In time you will come to know it," said Francis.

When they reached the lobby, Sophie was there waiting. She knew right away that Doug had died; the look on Mary Alice's face told it all.

"Are you okay?" she asked Mary Alice.

"I will be," answered Mary Alice as she tried her best to be strong. Her knees began to weaken, but she composed herself and stood tall. Unable to hide the devastation on her face or in her voice, she told her friend that Doug had died.

"I thought so," said Sophie. I'm so sorry. It's strange, because Julie started crying while we were having coffee. She leaned over and whispered something to David, then she hugged him. If I didn't know better, I'd say she knew when it happened and told David."

Sophie took Mary Alice by the hand and tried to lead her to a chair. "Come on over here and sit down."

"No, I just want to go home," said Mary Alice.

"Wait right here," said Sophie. "I'll get Lavern and Minnie. We'll take you home."

"No, I mean home to Mississippi," said Mary Alice. "Maybe if I had stayed there in the first place, none of this would have happened. I just can't stay here anymore. I need to go home."

"I understand," said Sophie. She went to get Lavern and Minnie to tell them about Doug.

"Everything's going to be all right," said Francis. "You just stay strong and trust in the Lord."

There was a certain comfort in all that Francis said, and Mary Alice wondered if she could be the angel her mother spoke of. Maybe the angel's name was Francis.

Minutes later, Sophie returned with Minnie, Lavern, and the kids, but without Jessie.

"We'll take the kids with us," said Lavern. "Jessie said he's going over to Charlie's and tell them what happened. He's having a real hard time with this. He's crying like a little baby, and you know how men don't want a woman to see them cry."

"Sam's the same way," said Minnie. "He cried when I told him about Edward. You know, that was the first time I ever saw him cry. I didn't know he had it in him."

For the first time in a long time Mary Alice smiled. It was good to know that her family was loved so much by so many.

"Let's go," said Minnie, ushering everyone toward the door.

"Jessie's going to talk to the men and see about making arrangements to get you back home," said Lavern. She stood there holding the door open.

"We'll be going with you," said Sophie.

"You know friends got to stick together," added Minnie.

Francis stood there, watching as Mary Alice was escorted from the hospital to the car. God's grace seemed to surround her. Her steps were once again sure and her stride was graceful. David finally let go of Julie's hand and reached for his mother. Mary Alice leaned down, picked him up, and held him tightly in her arms. He was all she had left, but God had made a promise to her. Through the angel, he had said that David would grow to be a leader among men and his greatness would be known throughout the land. This was the word from the Lord and in that she found comfort.

Francis watched as the car vanished into the distance. She stood there for a few long moments watching the traffic light change from red to green then back to red. Finally, she turned and walked over to the desk to make the necessary phone calls. After making the proper notifications and filling out the paperwork, she walked back upstairs to Doug's room.

The room was dark. Francis fell to her knees beside the bed and knelt there silently. She extended her hands, tilted her head back and closed her eyes. Then God spoke into the darkness and the darkness gave way to the light. With her assignment complete, the angel was gone, back to heaven and into the presence of the Lord.

CHAPTER XIII

The Lord will give strength unto his people;
The Lord will bless his people with peace.

Psalm 29:11

ews of Doug's death spread quickly and a sadness gripped the projects. On the street corners, in the stores, and at the bus stops, Doug's death was the topic of conversations. With the mention of Doug's death came talk of Mary Alice, of her boundless faith and of her visit from the angel. She became a symbol of all the pain and suffering that touches the lives of us all. She was a living example that God does answer prayers.

From the time she arrived home that afternoon, there was a constant stream of visitors to her tiny apartment. Everyone wanted to see her and hear about the angel that appeared to her at the hospital. Like Mary Alice, each of them at one time or another had experienced the devastation caused by the loss of a cousin, a friend, a parent, a child, or a spouse. For some, God had sent an angel to speak, for others he had spoken the words himself to ease the pain.

For Mitch the mailman, it was following the loss of his wife during the birth of their second child. God's intervention and the support of his friends was the only thing that kept him in his right mind. All that night and the next day following her death, he sat on the edge of his bed, not knowing how he would make it through the next day, the next hour, or the next minute. Just as he was about to let go, God reached out and grabbed him. He held him close and whispered to him, "Be still and know that I am God." The words and the sound of the voice would remain with him forever.

Five years later, he was still recovering from the loss of his partner in life, but through it all, God had given him the strength to hold on. Late at night, when his heart was heavy, he could still hear the words, "Be still and know that I am God."

For Flora, the school crossing guard, it was the devastation of losing her only sister at an early age. With no remaining family, she felt there was no justification for the Lord to take her sister from her. The night of her sister's death, Flora lay in bed, her faith in God fading and her life about to slip away. She fell to her knees and called out to the Lord.

"Be merciful to me Lord, for I am faint. My soul is in agony and my spirit is crushed. Where are you, my God, in this time of need? Will the pain never cease? Will the torment of my soul forever be with me? Will your grace no longer give me comfort? It is me Lord, it is me. Do you no longer know your faithful servant? Please Lord, speak to me."

She dropped her head to the floor and stretched her arms out in front of her. Just as she was about to let go, God reached out and grabbed her. He wrapped her in his arms and held her close so she couldn't let go. Then out of the darkness, the Angel of the Lord spoke to her. "The eyes of the Lord are on the righteous and his ears are attentive to their cry. The Lord has heard your cries and knows of your pain. You will come to see that weeping endures for a night but joy comes in the morning. From this night forward, your mornings will be filled with joy. God's grace will provide comfort and you will find peace. These things the Lord will provide to you, for you have kept his commandments and trusted in him. You have been a true and faithful servant, and for that you will be blessed. This is the word from the Lord." Then there was silence and the angel was gone back into heaven.

That morning, Flora again found joy in life. God's grace provided comfort and she found peace in the Lord.

So it was. Whether they came to pay their respect, to show their admiration, or merely out of curiosity, they came to the tiny apartment in the projects. They came to see Mary Alice and hear about the angel. For some, the devastation of their loss still consumed them. They wondered if God would ever hear their prayers and free them from the sorrow that haunted them both day and night. They needed answers. So, they too came.

Not everyone receives a visit from an angel, or hears a voice in the dark that stills their soul and gives them peace. For some, the grief is never-ending and the sorrow is constant. Where is God at a time like this for those tormented souls, and why does he not hear their cries? Have they angered God in some way? Are they bad people, or do bad things happen to good people for no apparent reason? Is life after death their reward for a life of faithfulness filled with sadness? If the afterlife is the reward for these good people, can their reward be consolation enough for the loved ones who are left behind to grieve? Can faith and the support of friends be enough to heal their broken hearts? Mary Alice showed that it could.

It was late afternoon before the last of the visitors finally left the apartment. Mary Alice was asleep on the couch. The children were in the bedroom pretending to do the same, all the while trying to hear what the adults were saying.

"Johnathan doesn't believe Mary Alice saw an angel," said Sophie. "He said women are just too emotional, and seeing an angel was a hysterical reaction to Doug's death. Excuse me. When Mary Magdalene saw Jesus at the empty tomb, was that a hysterical reaction? I don't think so. Listen, I believe with all my heart that Mary Magdalene saw Jesus at the tomb, and I believe God answered our prayers and sent an angel to that hospital to save Mary Alice."

"I don't know what's happened to Johnathan," she said. "It seems like his faith in God has all but left him. I'm starting to think that maybe it never was really there in the first place." She looked over at Mary Alice and lowered her voice as if she didn't want her or the children to hear what she was saying. "That child knows what she saw. God don't play games."

"If she said she saw an angel, then she saw an angel," said Minnie.

"That's what I been trying to tell Jessie," said Lavern. "Right now he's just confused. Deep down inside, he knows what Mary Alice saw. I just wish God would send an angel to talk to him. It's been hard on him, losing his best friend. It's like a part of him died when Edward died."

"It's been hard on everybody," said Sophie. "That's why I don't understand Johnathan. He acts like this is all just a part of life, and life goes on. The only thing that seems to matter to him is his job and making more money. I don't even seem important to him anymore, and girl, I use to be the one. I told him friends and family are what really matters, not money or jobs. We're supposed to help each other. That's what life is all about, helping each other."

Sophie stood and walked over to the door. She leaned against the doorframe and stared through the screen at the people still lingering outside. The sun would be setting soon and a hectic day would come to a close, but still the people came. Good people, caring people. She was touched by the prayers and the show of respect by all those who came. There was still goodness in life.

Her thoughts drifted back to her husband, and she wondered what happened to the goodness in their life. Johnathan wasn't always like this. What happened? Was it Ohio? Was it her? Maybe it was the accident and Edward's death. Maybe Ohio wasn't meant for them. Maybe they should have stayed in Mississippi. She turned and walked back to her seat and joined her friends.

"When I married Johnathan, I thought he was the most caring person in the world," she said. "I guess I was wrong. He's like a different person, especially since the accident and Edward's death. He even said he can't go back to Mississippi for the funeral. Talkin' about he gotta work. Ain't that something, he gotta work. Edward and Doug have died and he gotta work. I don't know if he just don't want to go back to Mississippi or if Edward's friendship wasn't that important. If nothing else, you'd think he would at least go with me out of respect."

"You just stay strong and hold on, honey," said Minnie. "This accident has affected everybody in a different way, but God has a way of making things right."

"Amen," said Lavern. "And don't you let that man worry you to death."

Sophie smiled. She knew what they meant. "I'll be all right," she said, but she wasn't so sure.

The kids had slid the two beds together and were sitting together in a small circle discussing what they had heard.

"Did your mother really see an angel?" asked John, Jr.

David didn't answer right away, so Julie answered for him. "Yes she did. It was the Angel of the Lord."

"What does he look like?" asked Alfred.

"Does he have wings?" asked David.

"He looks like the other angels," answered Julie. "Yes, he has wings and he wears a long white robe."

"Is he a black man or a white man?" asked John, Jr.

"You can't tell what color he is because of the light," said Julie. "Sometimes the angels on earth are black and sometimes they're white. Those are the ones who look just like regular people. Sometimes they're kids and sometimes they're old people. It just depends on what God wants them to do. God sends them here to help people when they're in trouble. That's why he sent the angels to the hospital."

David looked at Julie as if searching for something, maybe wings. "Did God send you to help me?" he asked.

Julie leaned over and hugged David before answering, "Yes he did."

A faint smile appeared on David's face but then he started to cry. Since the accident he would occasionally do that. Sometimes it was just too much for him. Just as a child's laughter is contagious, so is his sorrow. They all sat there with tears in their eyes, wrapped in his sorrow, as their little friend cried uncontrollably. Try as he might, David couldn't stop the flow of his tears. He was such a young child to lose so much.

Julie leaned over and hugged him again. "It's going to be all right," she said. "It's going to be all right."

"I want my daddy," he said. "I want to go back to Mississippi. I don't like it in Ohio. Why did we have to come here, anyway? I wish we could have stayed in Mississippi on the farm."

"It's okay," said John, Jr.

"Yeah," said Alfred as they all moved closer to David. He was their friend and they all felt his pain. Their closeness and encouragement gave him the strength to at least stop the tears. He wiped his eyes and looked up at his friends.

"Why did God take my daddy and my brother?" he asked.

John, Jr. and Alfred didn't know what to say, but Julie did. She looked at each of them then asked David, "Do you love the Lord and trust in him?"

"Yes I do," he answered.

"Then I want to tell you a story," she said. They all moved closer and waited. "A long, long time ago in the land of Uz, there lived a great man whose name was Job. Job was God's favorite. God gave him lots of kids and made him very rich. One day, the angels came to see the Lord and the Devil was with them."

"Is the Devil real?" interrupted Alfred.

"Yes he is," answered Julie. "Do you believe in God?"

"Yes I do," said Alfred.

"Then if you believe in God, you have to believe in the Devil," explained Julie. "Anyway, the Devil didn't like Job because Job loved the Lord. The Devil asked the Lord to take away everything Job had, to see if Job would still love him."

By now Julie had their undivided attention. They had never heard of Job and the story captivated them. Julie paused for a moment, then continued, "So the Lord took away everything Job had."

"Did he take away his kids?" asked David.

"Yes," answered Julie. "All of them. Their house fell on them and they all died."

There was a collective gasp from her little audience. They looked at each other, then back at Julie and waited for her to continue. Julie looked around, then lowered her voice as if revealing a secret. "God took away everything. He took all of his camels and his sheep and his donkeys. Then God made Job very sick and he almost died. Job took off his robe and sat down in the ashes and he cried. He was very sad. Once he was a great man, but now he had lost everything. He lost his family. All that he had left was his wife and he almost lost her.

"Job's three closest friends heard what happened to him and they came to see him, to give him comfort. You see, David is like Job and, we are like Job's three friends."

They all glanced at David, who once again had tears in his eyes. David thought of Job losing all of his children. He thought of his own father, of his brother. He thought of the pain his mother must be experiencing and, like Job, he began to cry.

"What did Job's friends do?" asked John, Jr., wondering what they could do to comfort their friend.

Julie looked at David. She started to offer some words of comfort but decided to continue on with the story.

"When Job's friends saw him, they sat down on the ground in the ashes with him and they cried too."

"How long did they sit there?" asked David.

"They sat there with him for seven days and seven nights," answered Julie. "Nobody said a word, because they knew Job was very, very sad. After seven days Job spoke. He spoke to God and wished he had never been born.

"God answered. His answers made Job realized that whatever God decides to do, He is right. He realized that God does what he does because he is God. He realized God's true greatness. Even though God had taken everything Job had, Job loved God anyway. He knew that God was too great to understand."

"Did God send an angel to Job?" asked David.

"Nope," answered Julie. "God spoke to Job himself. Finally, everyone who knew Job came to his house to visit him. They all gave him money. Then God blessed Job with twice as much as he had before. He also blessed Job with seven sons and three daughters. His daughters were the most beautiful in the land. God made Job a great man again, and Job lived to be one-hundred and forty years old."

"Wow," said Alfred. "That's really old."

Julie paused, then looked at David. "You have to be like Job. God does things for a reason. I don't know why God took your father and your brother. Job didn't know why God took his children and everything he had, but he trusted God and still loved him. Whatever God takes from your life, he will replace it with something else. One day when you grow up, you will be like Job. You will be a great man. You will be known throughout the land, but you have to love the Lord and always, always trust him. Now promise me you will."

"I will," answered David. "I promise."

"Everything's going to be all right," said Julie.

"I know," said David. He smiled and all of his friends smiled with him.

CHAPTER XIV

If you do not stand firm in your faith you will not stand at all.

Isaiah 7:9

Coltrane's saxophone played softly in the background as Sam, Jessie, Johnathan, and Charlie sat in the record shop reminiscing about their late friend. Charlie's had become the gathering place for a variety of good music and conversation about a multitude of subjects, but today was different. Today the conversation was about one subject and the music by one artist. Talk centered around Edward, and all day long Coltrane's saxophone was the music of choice. That was all Edward ever wanted to hear and today, that was all Charlie played. "Catch the A Train" was playing for the third time and no one complained.

"He never wanted much," said Jessie. "All he ever wanted was that old Hudson and a fair chance in life. I think God called the wrong name when he pulled Edward's number. It just don't seem fair."

Edward's death had dealt Jessie a hard blow and he was having trouble dealing with it. Sometimes life does that. It will test your faith when you are least prepared and Jessie just wasn't prepared. He stood, walked over, and leaned against the counter next to Charlie. He stared out of the window as if there might be something out there to ease his pain, but there was nothing.

"Can you play "Blue Train"?" he finally asked. "I like Lee Morgan on that one and it was one of Edward's favorites."

"I think I can do that," said Charlie. "Johnnie B. liked that one too. He liked Paul Chambers on bass, but I'm like you; I'm kinda partial to Lee Morgan's trumpet."

And so it went. Talk of Edward, along with Coltrane's music, carried them into the evening. As the daylight faded to dusk, Johnathan walked over to the door and gazed out at the approaching darkness. He stood there, thinking of Edward and their days in Mississippi together. He thought of Mary Alice and wondered what could she have done for God to inflict such terrible suffering on her. He thought of the late night visit from the police officer who told them of the accident and Edward's death. He thought of his wife and how she cried for her friend. He hung his head and closed his eyes, wishing it would all just go away. Reaching out, he switched on the lights for the outdoor sign.

"Can't you play something else?" he asked. He had grown tired of the somber mood and Coltrane's wailing saxophone.

He walked back to his seat and sat down. He leaned back in the chair with his head against the wall and thought of how things had been in Mississippi. He thought of Doug playing with his son, of the wives laughing and cooking together. He thought of Edward's old Hudson and the countless hours they spent working on it. He would miss his friend, but he knew it was time to get on with his life. It was time for them all to get on with life. This too would pass and one day it would all be just a memory. He raised his head and looked around as if waking from a dream.

"A man died and everybody's sitting around like the world has come to an end. I know Edward was our friend, but life goes on," he said.

Jessie, irritated by the remark, reached behind the counter and turned the music down just enough to make sure he would be heard when he spoke."If he really was your friend, you wouldn't be talking like that. At least show some respect. Seems like you can't even find time to go to your friend's funeral. You got to work! I guess money is more important than friendship." He hesitated, but before Johnathan could respond, Jessie continued, "A good man died in that accident and God took away a child. Mary Alice lost half of her family, and you tellin' me that life goes on! Goes on for who?!" He glared at Johnathan as if to blame him, not only for the accident, but for all the problems of the free world.

"Goes on for who?!" he repeated, this time a little louder than necessary.

"Take it easy," said Charlie as he grabbed Jessie by the arm.

"I'm sorry," said Jessie. He pulled his arm away but continued to stare at Johnathan.

"Life goes on for all of us," answered Johnathan. "Look man, don't get me wrong. Edward was my friend too, but going to that funeral won't pay my bills. I got a job to keep and money to make. God will take care of Edward, but I got to take care of me. You think God's gonna pay my rent or buy my groceries? God's only gonna do so much. The rest is up to me. Sure I feel sorry for Mary Alice, but things happen and they happen because of the choices we make. God gave us free will. The ability to choose. Maybe Edward and Mary Alice should have chose to stay in Mississippi. Who knows? Maybe they angered God in some way or maybe they disobeyed him. I don't know. I don't know why God did what he did. I guess he got his reasons. But, somebody did something wrong for God to take Edward and the child. Maybe God's punishing Mary Alice. Who knows? Maybe she did something wrong. Maybe she should have stayed in Mississippi."

Sam climbed down from his chair and walked over to the cooler to get a drink. He didn't want to hear anymore of

Johnathan's misplaced logic. "Mississippi had nothing to do with Edward's death," he said. "It was an accident, plain and simple. It makes no difference where he was. Edward could have stayed in Mississippi and it wouldn't have mattered. When God decides it's your time to go, it's your time to go."

He stood in front of the cooler trying to decide what he wanted to drink. More than that, he was thinking about what Johnathan had just said. Maybe he was right. Maybe Edward's death was punishment for some sin. Why else would God take such a good man and a child? Should the child be punished for the sins of a parent? Things like that weren't suppose to happen. Sam just didn't understand.

"Get a grape and get me one too," said Mr. Washington, helping Sam decide on a drink but knowing what was really on his mind.

"How about getting me an orange?" said Jessie.

"Me too," said Johnathan. "I'll have the same."

"Who's paying for all this?" asked Sam. "You know I don't have any money." He grabbed a handful of drinks from the cooler and laughed.

"Charlie's paying," said Jessie, and the mood lightened considerably. "Charlie's got all the money. If he can pay for everybody's ticket back to Mississippi and pay for the funeral, he can certainly buy a few cold drinks." There was laughter and thanks all around as they raised their bottles and toasted Charlie.

The train tickets had been purchased by Charlie. There would be no funeral, just a simple graveside service attended by Edward's closest friends and their families. Edward and Doug would be buried on the property in Mississippi. That's how he would have wanted it, and that's all Mary Alice had asked for. Paying for everything had been an easy decision for Charlie. Over time, he came to realize that he didn't have money because he was lucky or smart. He had it because he was blessed, and if you're blessed, you should be a blessing to others. Like Johnnie B., he had more than enough money, and what better way to spend it than helping his friends, he thought.

Johnathan thought work was his blessing, and he was going to make all the money he could. Friendship was a distant second. To Charlie, money instead of friendship was not a good trade. Eventually, any fool will have some money. He laughed to himself, realizing he was a good example of that.

The music ended and Coltrane's saxophone finally fell silent. Mr. Washington reached under one of the chairs for his shoeshine box. He opened it and removed the tools of his trade, then took a long drink from his soda. He looked at the group of men gathered around him, trying to comfort each other over the loss of their friend. They reminded him of Job's friends, trying to comfort him after he had lost all that he had. They're intentions were good but they only made things worse. Mr. Washington took another long drink from his soda, then handed the almost empty bottle to back to Sam.

"Here, do something with this," he said. Sam smiled, shook his head and did as he was told. They all gave Mr. Washington his well-deserved respect and granted his every request, usually without question.

"Thanks," said the little shoeshine man. He reached into the pouch of his apron and pulled out his ever-present Bible. "You boys read this book lately?" he asked.

"Come on," said Johnathan. We don't need a sermon today."

"I beg to differ," said Mr. Washington. The angel in him wanted to surface, but first there were some things his little congregation needed to understand. Most of all, they needed to understand what life was really about. They needed to understand that life is about more than staying in Mississippi or coming to Ohio. And that it's about more than a job. It's about more than making money or losing a friend. They needed to understand that it's about more than having free will and making your own choices, and it's certainly about more than John Coltrane's saxophone.

They needed to understand that life is about faith. It's about believing and knowing that whatever happens in life, a person's faith must remain strong. It must. He looked at Jessie whose faith had been shattered. He looked at Sam who wondered if the death of Edward and Doug was punishment from God for some sin. He looked at Johnathan who mistakenly thought that he could make it through life alone, that faith or true friendship was not a requirement. He looked at Charlie and just smiled.

They all needed to understand that life is about family and friendship. It's about knowing that when difficult times arrive, those are the people who will be there. They are the ones who will pray with you, laugh with, you and cry with you. They are the support system that is so crucial in overcoming life's obstacles and keeping one's faith.

It's about the necessity of living life to the fullest. They needed to understand that time on earth is short and each moment is precious. It's about enjoying each moment in order to accept life's end, whether that end be theirs or that of a loved one. It's about living in such a way that when the end does come, you will be grateful for having experienced the gift of life.

They needed to understand that it's about the awesome power of prayer. Everyone, at some point in their life will be helped through a difficult time by the prayers of others. Those prayers will make it possible to stay the course, keep the faith, and maintain one's sanity during life's most tragic moments.

"Look at you," said Mr. Washington. All of you, coming here confused, crying on each other's shoulders, and trying to understand why God did this or why God let that happen. You standing here, not knowing what life is all about and wanting answers. You want answers, but the answers you want are based on faith, and that's what you don't have enough of." He paused, but only for a moment, then continued, "Your wives found the answers that you're searching for because they have faith. They have an undying faith. They have a deep love for God, for each other, and for you. Because of that faith and that love, when they cried out to the Lord, he heard their cries. God answered them by sending down his angels." He looked directly at Jessie and repeated himself. "By sending down his angels!"

Mr. Washington paused again, remembering how God and the angels listened as Mary Alice's friends prayed for her. He remembered how he cried along with the rest of the angels when Doug died. He remembered Francis, kneeling on that cold hospital floor, crying out to God. He remembered God, wrapping Mary Alice in his arms to keep her from slipping away. He remembered the Angel of the Lord being sent to earth as God's answer to their prayers and their cries. Tears started to form in his eyes at the recollection of it all, but they were tears of joy—joy, because Mary Alice and her friends understood what some people never would understand. They understood the awesome power of prayer. He looked at their husbands and hoped that they too would one day understand what was truly important in life.

"Your wives discovered what's important in life," he said. "One day, may you discover the same peace, experience the same joy, and find the same strength of spirit that they have found. May you come to know, as they do, what prayer can accomplish if you just believe. May you too come to understand and appreciate all that you have been blessed with."

The four of them stood there, staring at the angelic little shoeshine man. They understood all they had heard, or at least they thought they did. Jessie came to believe that Mary Alice had actually been visited by an angel at the hospital. He smiled and realized that he probably was in the presence of an angel at that very moment.

Johnathan realized that he did have true friends and Edward had been one of them. He realized that their friendship was worth a lot more than a few extra dollars. So, he decided that even if he had to buy his own ticket and miss work, he would be on that train to Mississippi to bury his friend. Work and money could wait. His rent would be paid and his family would have food regardless. God would provide.

For Charlie, it just confirmed all that he had learned since leaving Mississippi: life for him was good. Like Johnnie B., he knew that he was only on this earth for a very short time. So, he lived life to the fullest and celebrated each and every moment of it. He appreciated and shared with his friends all that he had been blessed with. He learned to truly love the Lord. He did all of this because God had been good to him and he knew it.

As for Sam, he had always believed. Standing there with his friends and Mr. Washington, he was simply glad he came to Ohio and had the opportunity to meet this magical little shoeshine man. His faith had been restored and, once again, he realized that life truly was good. Even though he would miss Edward, he knew that it was God's will and not punishment for some sin. He knew that God answered their prayers and all was well.

Mr. Washington placed his Bible back in the pouch of his apron. He sat down on the little ledge in front of the chairs, bowed his head, and closed his eyes. They all gathered around him and did the same. No one said a word and Coltrane's saxophone remained silent. All were lost in their own thoughts, but silently giving thanks for the same reasons. They gave thanks for the same reasons that we should all give thanks. We should give thanks for our family, for our friends, and for our blessings. Most of all, we should give thanks for God's mercy and his grace. Through his mercy he doesn't give us what we deserve, but through his grace he gives us what we don't deserve: his forgiveness, his blessings and his love.

Finally, Mr. Washington opened his eyes and looked at his watch. "Gentlemen, it's getting late. I've got some packing to do if I'm going to be on that train with you tomorrow night for Mississippi. I'm an old man and I need my rest, so I'd better get started."

He stood and began placing the tools of his trade back into the shoeshine box. After each item had been put in its proper place, he removed his apron and folded it across his arm. With a departing tip of his cap, the little shoeshine man turned and walked toward the door leading to the stairs. Shoeshine box in hand, he started up the stairs to his apartment. They watched him go and listened as the sound of his footsteps faded into silence.

"What time does the train leave?" asked Johnathan.

Charlie looked at Johnathan and smiled. He pulled a ticket from the inside pocket of his jacket and gave it to Johnathan.

"Here, all the information is on your ticket," he said. "I thought you might be needing this."

Johnathan looked at his friends, then slowly shook his head, ashamed of what he had said earlier. Sometimes words cannot describe what a person feels. For Johnathan, this was one of those times. So, he simply extended his hand and hoped they would understand. Among friends a handshake sometimes says it all.

"Thanks," he said. I owe you all an apology." They all reached out in turn and shook Johnathan's hand.

"It's all right," said Jessie. "It's been a strain on everybody. It's tough losing a friend. You never know how much a person means to you until they're gone. I loved that man like a brother and I never took the time to tell him."

"We all loved him," said Johnathan. He tried his best not to get too emotional. He was not the kind to openly show his feelings, and right now that was not easy. "I've got to go." He folded the ticket, placed it in his pocket, then turned to leave. He just wanted to go home and hug John, Jr. and Sophie. He owed her an apology and he knew that she would require more than a handshake.

"We all better go," said Sam. "It'll be time to catch that train before we know it. Let's get together tomorrow and have some dinner before we go. It'll be on me."

They all gladly agreed.

Charlie walked them to the door, switched off the lights, and put up the closed sign. He watched his friends as they headed for the cars. He stood there, alone in the darkness of his shop, thinking of Edward and Johnnie B. He missed his friends. He walked up the stairs to his apartment, realizing what was truly important in life.

Late the next evening, they all met at the train station for dinner. After dinner, just before midnight, they boarded the train for Mississippi.

CHAPTER XV

The grace of the Lord Jesus be with God's people, Amen.

The train ride back to Mississippi had been long and exhausting. For the children, the late night departure and the layover in Chicago made the trip all the more difficult. Late on Friday night, they arrived in Jackson, Mississippi. Once there, they immediately boarded a bus for Starkville.

Mary Alice gazed out of the window of the bus as it made its way through the countryside. This was home, and she wondered if she should have ever left. Would Edward and Doug be alive today if she had stayed in Mississippi? Could this whole tragedy somehow have been prevented? Was she in some way responsible for their deaths? She closed her eyes and listened to the sound of the gravel as the bus made its way down the rocky road towards Starkville. She missed that sound. She missed her husband and she missed her son.

For David, just being back in Mississippi was worth the journey. He had gone from cars to horses and from streets to dirt roads. This was home and he was sure they should have never left. He turned and caught a glimpse of his mother's reflection in the window and wondered if she was awake.

"Momma." he whispered. "Are you asleep?"

"No, is something wrong. Are you all right?" She put her arm around his shoulder and gently pulled him to her. "What's wrong, honey?"

He sat there, almost afraid to hear the answers to the questions he was about to ask. "Are we going home or does somebody else live in our house?"

Mary Alice pulled him a little closer then kissed him on top of his head. "We're going to spend the night with Sam and Minnie then we'll go home tomorrow. It's still our home."

"Are the horses still there?" he asked.

"Yes they are," she answered.

"Good. I want to learn to ride Old Cliff." He smiled, then rested his head on her lap.

They both drifted off to sleep as the bus turned onto the two-lane blacktop and continued on to Starkville.

Charlie had made arrangements for the bus to take them directly to the church when they arrived in Starkville. From there, Reverend Johnson and people from the congregation would provide transportation to Sam and Minnie's where Mary Alice and David would spend the night. The caskets had been shipped to the funeral home and the burial would take place the next day.

A gentle tap on Mary Alice's shoulder, followed by the soft whisper of a familiar voice, woke her from her sleep. It was Lavern.

"Wake up, girl" she said. "We're almost there."

Mary Alice rubbed her eyes and stretched. She looked down at David and decided to let him get a few more minutes of sleep.

"How you feeling?" asked Lavern.

"I feel okay," answered Mary Alice. "Just a little tired."

"That's two of us," said Lavern.

Minutes later, the bus turned onto a secluded dirt road, then up a long driveway. Soon it stopped in front of the church.

141

"Here we are, folks" said Sam. "Home again."

One by one they filed from the bus while Reverend Johnson stood at the bottom of the steps greeting them with a handshake. As he shook their hands, his eyes scanned the doorway looking for Mary Alice. Finally she appeared at the top of the steps. Reverend Johnson helped her off of the bus, then he hugged her and she hugged him. For a few long moments they held each other and not a word was said. Finally he pushed her back slightly and looked at her as if she were his prodigal child returning home. He took Mary Alice by the hand and carried David to the car. He helped her in and lay David down across the back seat. They drove off with the other cars following.

"I know what happened in Ohio," said Reverend Johnson. "Are you okay?"

"I will be," answered Mary Alice.

"How's David doing?" he asked. "He's been through an awful lot for a child so young."

"He seems to be doing better," she said. "He had a real hard time at first. Now he doesn't talk about it at all. Julie's helped a lot. It's as if she were an angel sent by God just to save David." She thought of Doug and how the angels didn't or couldn't save him. She thought of how her own life almost slipped away. She thought of Edward and all that he wanted them to have. She thought of all the dreams that would never be realized and of her child who died so young. She thought of all that had happened and she began to cry. Tears began to form in her eyes and she covered her face with both hands. Unable to contain her emotions, she leaned her head against Reverend Johnson's shoulder and cried uncontrollably.

"It's going to be all right," said Reverend Johnson. He handed her his handkerchief and asked God to give her strength. They rode on in silence. The only sound was the occasional sobbing of Mary Alice as she tried to regain her composure. After a few minutes, she sat up and dried her eyes.

"I'm sorry," she said. "Sometimes, it's all just too much. You'd think by now I'd be all cried out, but I don't think that will ever happen." She looked over her shoulder at David as if to make sure he was asleep before she continued. "An angel came to me in Akron at the hospital when Doug died," she whispered. She sat there, staring at Reverend Johnson and waiting for some reaction, some response, some words of wisdom, something. There was nothing.

Finally, he spoke. "I know. It was the Angel of the Lord. You asked questions of God, and he sent the angel to give you answers. You have favor with the Lord. Even through your suffering, you are being blessed. Listen, when Doug died angels everywhere cried and prayed for you. God listened. He hears the cries of the brokenhearted and he knows their pain. He hears their prayers and answers those prayers. He commanded his angels to guard you and David in all your ways. David will grow to be a leader among men and be known throughout the land. You will come to be blessed far more than you ever dreamed. You will become an example of the power of prayer. This is the word from the Lord."

Mary Alice looked at Reverend Johnson and wondered how he could possibly know these things. She knew he was a man of God. *Maybe he knows because he's a preacher,* she thought. She sat there, quiet and confused, not sure what to think. One thing she knew for sure was that God keeps his word. She would stay in Mississippi and wait on the Lord. Edward and Doug would be buried on the property down by the pond. When her days on earth were through, her final resting place would be with them.

Reverend Johnson turned from the road and stopped in front of Sam and Minnie's house and the other cars pulled in behind them. He stepped from the car and walked around to the passenger side to help Mary Alice out.

"Let me help you with David," she said. He's kind of heavy."

"Nonsense, child," said Reverend Johnson. "I'm old, but not that old. I can still bear the weight of a child."

He leaned over and picked David up and carried him into the house. It was quite a struggle this time, but he managed. The women came in with the rest of the kids while the men carried the luggage. Reverend Johnson shook hands with the men and kissed each of the women and children on the cheek. He whispered a few words to Mr. Washington then turned to leave.

"I've got to go," he said. "All the arrangements have been made, and the people from the funeral home will be by early tomorrow morning to take you to the farm for the burial." As he passed by Mary Alice, he took her by the arm and led her outside. "God has started a great work through you," he said. He started to say more but stopped. He gave her a quick hug and walked to his car. He seemed tired. The death of Edward and Doug had taken its toll on him. For an earthly angel, nothing is sadder or more heartfelt than the death of a good person and the passing of a child. He sat in the car for a few long moments staring up at the sky, then he slowly drove away.

Mary Alice watched as the lights of the car disappeared into the darkness. She went back inside and put David in bed with the other kids. She got her Bible and a blanket then lay down on the couch. She covered herself with the blanket then went to sleep with her Bible in her hand.

Early that morning, just after sunrise, people began gathering near the woods on Mary Alice's farm. From all over Oktibbeha County they came. They came to pay their respect to a good man and to a child who died so young. They came to see the woman who, like Job, held on to her faith even after losing so much. They came because they knew the Lord was in that place.

To them, Mary Alice had become a living example of the power of prayer. She stood for anyone who had lost a husband or a wife. She represented those who had lost a parent or a child, or those who had a friend suddenly taken from them. One man thought of his only brother who died during the war and he cried. He cried because, like everyone there, he knew how great Mary Alice's suffering was.

Mary Alice had decided to walk to the farm with Minnie, Lavern, and Sophie. The men rode in the limousine to serve as pallbearers. The children, unable to resist a walk through the woods, joined their mothers. Once there, Mary Alice made her way through the crowd to her little bench by the pond. She sat down with her arm around David and her head leaning on Sophie's shoulder. Lavern and Minnie stood behind her, ready to offer any support that might be needed.

As for David, the fear was gone. There was no longer a fear of monsters in the woods. He realized that there were no monsters, only angels, and that those angels would always be here to watch over his father and brother. He leaned against his mother, secure in the fact that those same angels would always watch over him.

It was as if the entire county had come to the pond by the woods to join Mary Alice and her friends. They came to celebrate the life of a good man and the life of a child. Reverend Johnson said a few words, but mostly it was a time of reflection and prayer. There were no long speeches or testimonials, just friends gathered together to pray for a friend.

Early that afternoon, the last prayer was said and the caskets were lowered into the ground. As was his custom, Reverend Johnson silently asked God to bless and protect this congregation.

"Amen," he said as if he had prayed out loud.

"Amen," repeated his congregation as if they had heard him pray.

Reverend Johnson raised his hands and in a voice that echoed through the trees, he almost shouted, "When two or three are gathered in my name, there I am with them." He looked out over the crowd gathered there and he knew that the Lord was in this place.

He lowered his arms and his voice, then dismissed the crowd.

Slowly, almost reluctantly, people started for home. When the last of the crowd had left, Mary Alice sent David home with Lavern, leaving just her and Reverend Johnson there. They talked for a while about the past and all that had happened. He told her of God's plans for her and David. He told her of the direction their lives would take and that God always keeps his word.

Mary Alice listened intently as Reverend Johnson repeated all that the Angel of the Lord had told her. After he finished, Mary Alice assured him that she would be all right. He hugged her then turned and left.

She sat there on the bench, alone with her thoughts. Looking down, she stared at the two graves, unwilling or unable to let go. Where was her angel, she wondered. Where was God? She needed him. Tears filled her eyes and she fell to her knees and prayed for a word from the Lord. She raised her hands to the sky and cried out to God for strength. Once again, God heard her cries. This time, however, there was no flash of light or appearance of an angel. God merely granted her request. He gave her strength. He gave her the strength to stand, the strength to dry her tears, and the strength to accept his will. More importantly, he gave her the strength to understand.

She stood, laid a flower across each grave, then headed home. Twice she started to turn back, but she continued on. She felt tired and needed some rest. Once she reached the house, she went straight to bed and cried herself to sleep. She slept until early the next morning when Lavern brought David home.

The angel never appeared to Mary Alice again, but the image and the words would remain with her forever. They would be an inspiration and a constant reminder to her of what was and what was to come.

That night, after putting David to bed, she walked outside and stood on the porch. She leaned against the support pole and stared up at the star-filled sky. It was an unusually warm night, but a gentle breeze and the clear skies made it very pleasant. She took off her shoes and sat down on the porch with her feet hanging over the edge. It was something she had done since she was a child, something that Edward had constantly teased her about. He would tell her that she was just a little old country girl. He was right. She was just a little old country girl. A little old country girl who loved her husband and her children very, very much.

When Edward died, a part of Mary Alice died with him. She would smile, but her smile would never again be as bright. She would laugh, but she would never again be as carefree. She would love, but her spirit would never again be joined with another and be as one. They had been partners in life, and without her partner, her life would never be the same. There would be peace, but at such a terrible price.

But God is a generous God, and Mary Alice had yet to realize that he always gives more than he takes. Even as she sat there, God was taking the broken pieces of her life and making it whole again. As the potter molds the clay, he was making her into more than she was before. She would be stronger. She would be wiser and she would be blessed far more than she had ever dreamed.

She stood up, put on her shoes, and walked over to the gate that led to the pasture. From the gate she could see the barn and the path that led to the pond down by the woods. She opened the gate then closed it behind her. She stood there, staring out over the pasture into the darkness, barely able to see the outline of the trees. She hesitated before following the path across the pasture to the woods. Once there, she sat down on the little bench by the pond that she and Edward had so often shared. She sat there gazing up at the stars. She noticed how quiet Mississippi was. It was almost too quiet. A soft breeze blew through the trees and somewhere in the distance a cricket chirped. She listened, then realized that Mississippi wasn't too quiet; Ohio had just been too noisy and was such a long ways from home. This was home and this was how it should be.

After all that happened to her, the storm had finally passed and she was at peace. In life's journey she had traveled far from where she started. The road had been rough and the journey difficult. Along the way she learned that weeping endures for a night but joy comes in the morning. She learned that life is to be lived and appreciated because of the suddenness with which it can be taken away. She learned the value of true friends and that true love never dies. Most importantly, she learned that prayers are answered , if you just believe.

Deep down inside of us all there is a strength that is seldom called on, but it is there. Mary Alice called on hers, and through prayer she found it. At that point, her life began anew and she once again found happiness in life. She came to realize all of this because God had been good to her and she knew it.

The grace of the Lord Jesus be with God's people.

Somebody say amen.

THE END

CPSIA information can be obtained at www.ICGtesting.com
Printed in the USA
BVOW041944120912

300303BV00005B/76/P